CRASH

A STONE KINGS MC ROMANCE

DAPHNE LOVELING

This book is a work of fiction.

Any similarity to persons living or dead is purely coincidental.

CONTENTS

DEDICATION

To Michelle and Dave, for their good counsel on all things regarding fundamentalist communities.

To anyone who has ever taken a leap of faith.

.

CHAPTER 1

Cherish

"Hurry up, Cherish, we're going to be late!" Sarah squealed from the bedroom doorway. "Father's waiting!"

I smiled in spite of myself as I coiled my long auburn hair into the severe bun that was my daily hairstyle, securing it with pin after pin so that no stray locks would find their way loose.

"Late for what?" I teased her, turning to inspect the twelve year-old girl and the three younger siblings who stood impatiently next to her. "Your father's not going to leave without us, you know." I was sure my quaking voice would betray the nervousness behind my lighthearted tone, but none of them seemed to notice anything out of the ordinary.

A groan escaped Abigail, the second oldest of the four children at ten years old. Her perpetually solemn face was twisted into a scowl of frustration. "We're never going to get to Coraza," she grumbled.

I opened my mouth automatically to chastise her for speaking immodestly, but shut it again without saying anything. In truth, I could hardly blame any of the children for being impatient. It was so rare that we ever got to leave the compound, much less venture into even a medium-sized town like Coraza. The prospect of a whole afternoon to roam the streets and glimpse the outside world must have been a much-awaited holiday from daily life for all of them.

Besides, I didn't want my interactions with them today to be anything but loving and kind. Not today.

I finished securing my hair and crossed to the far side of the room, risking a final nervous glance inside the covered basket I had prepared for the trip.

Finally, Aaron, the youngest, could stand it no more. "Come *on*, Cherish!" he whined, moving forward into the room to grab my hand and tug it toward the door. At five years old, he still had the pink, chubby cheeks of his toddler-hood, but his form had already begun to lengthen as he grew taller, and I could see hints of the boy he would be three or four years from now. A sharp tug at my heartstrings surprised me at the thought, almost making me rethink my plan. *No*, I steeled myself. *Don't lose courage now. This is your only chance.*

Securing the basket under my arm, I allowed myself to be led out of the room and toward the front door. The other children rushed ahead, blazing an excited path in front of us. Outside, the white minivan was waiting, inside it the children's father, Isaiah.

My husband.

I opened the sliding side door and the children piled in, making my face a mask of solemnity in their father's presence as I had been taught. Once I had slammed the door shut, I opened the passenger door and got in, being careful to place the basket unobtrusively by my feet.

"It's about time," Isaiah growled. "There's no call

for you dawdling."

I didn't answer. There was no point. Anything I said would only serve to anger him. I had learned that from bitter experience.

We rode along in silence, with only the occasional subdued whisper from one child to another. The trip into town took almost half an hour, and I stared out the window as we rode. This was where I had grown up, and where I had spent all of my almost twenty-two years. In some ways, I knew the landscape like the back of my hand, having ridden along this road hundreds of times before. But in other ways, it was as though the scrub and red sands of the mesa passing us by were a landscape I had only seen in a movie about someone else's life. I tried not to think about anything, to clear my head completely of both the sorrows of my past and the uncertainty of my future.

Soon enough, we arrived in town, and the younger ones piled out of the back of the van as I modestly stepped down from the front seat. I tucked my basket under my arm and stood patiently as the children assembled in a line next to me at the curb. Finally, Isaiah came around to speak to me.

"I'll be occupied over at Joseph Stubbs's place,"

he said sternly, looking only at me. "Be back here at two o'clock." Three hours. I had at least three hours before anyone would suspect anything, if I was lucky.

I nodded looking down at the ground in a gesture of submission. "Yes, Isaiah," I murmured.

My husband turned on his heel and headed off down the street. As soon as he was out of earshot, the children began clamoring their agendas and begging for treats. "Can we stop for ice cream?" asked Matthew hopefully, his eyes beseeching mine.

"Of course," I nodded, a lump rising in my throat. This was exactly what I had been planning to do, and yet, now with the reality of it facing me, I almost lost my nerve at the thought of leaving my four stepchildren with their father. An argument that I had had with myself a thousand times flooded me with doubts, but I pushed them away with resolve. I had made my decision. There was no turning back now.

"We'll go to Clancy's," I suggested, nodding my head in that direction.

"I like Maybelle's better," Abigail frowned, pointing at the gaily colored pink-and white storefront across the street.

"We're going to Clancy's," I said firmly. "It's closer to the shops I need to go to. You four can sit and have your ice cream while I run my errands."

A couple of the children grumbled, but the prospect of having unsupervised free-time and ice cream meant that they couldn't sustain their bad mood, and by the time we arrived at Clancy's, the younger ones were practically bouncing with joy. We walked into the ice cream parlor, a wall of cool, air-conditioned air hitting us as we went through the door. I closed my eyes for a moment to savor the feeling. I was unaccustomed to air conditioning, and it felt heavenly given the itchy, figure-concealing dress that all women of the WTZ Ranch were obligated to wear.

I stood in line with the children, waiting patiently as they hemmed and hawed over their selections as though the decision meant life or death. "Are you *sure* we can have anything we want?" asked Matthew, wide-eyed. Usually, on the rare occasions that the children were allowed an ice cream treat, they were limited to a small cone with no extras. But today I wanted to give them something special. Something I hoped they would remember one day: a small kindness by the woman who had deserted them without so much as a goodbye.

"Yes, anything," I smiled. "As long as it's meant for only one person."

Finally, after much deliberating, all of the children had ordered and received their treats. I told Sarah to get the children seated while I paid, and then I went over to the booth they had chosen, close to a window with cheerful sun streaming through.

I drew a deep breath. "All right, children," I said, trying to sound as normal as possible. "You stay right here and finish your treats. I have errands to run."

"Aren't you going to get ice cream, too?" inquired Aaron as he attacked a hot fudge sundae that was much too large for him.

"No, I'm not hungry," I replied. At least that much was true. My stomach was doing flips and flops as though it was trying to leap out of my throat. "Sarah, you keep an eye on the children for me, you hear?"

"M-hm," Sarah said dreamily as she took a spoonful of her malt, then realized she had been impertinent. "Yes, ma'am," she corrected herself.

I smiled, and suddenly I felt as though I might cry. I swallowed hard and blinked my eyes. "You children be good," I said, willing my voice not to crack. I touched little Aaron's blond head one last time, and left the ice cream parlor.

Outside, I turned right and walked hurriedly the few blocks toward my destination. Once I arrived in the noisy terminal, I strode as quickly and unobtrusively as I could toward the bathroom. Mercifully, no one was in it, and I went to the large handicapped stall, shut the door, and quickly stripped off my clothing. Opening the basket, I took out the worn, faded jeans I had purchased at the Goodwill on our last trip into town, and an ill-fitting yellow T-shirt that said, "One in a Minion," with a picture of a strange, bespectacled cartoon figure that I recognized and seemed popular. I hoped it would somehow make me look less conspicuous. Finally, I kicked off my hot, heavy shoes and exchanged them for a pair of cheap flip flop sandals that I had chosen because they would take the least amount of room in the basket. It made me feel uncomfortable having my bare feet so exposed, but I told myself that I didn't have time to fret about such things now.

When I had finished, I exited the stall and stuffed the clothes I had been wearing at the bottom of a large wastebasket by the door, covering them over with paper towels. I turned to the door to go, but decided to give myself a quick check in the mirror, and was horrified to discover that I was still wearing the tight bun that marked me unmistakably as from the WFZ Ranch. I began to sweat as I quickly removed pin after pin from my hair as fast as I could, until finally, they were all out and my long, uncut hair hung loose to my waist. I frowned at my reflection. I knew young "worldly" women didn't wear their hair like this. An idea came to me then, and I went back to the wastebasket and rooted around until I found one of my shoes. I quickly undid the lace and tied my hair back with it in an approximation of a loose ponytail that hid its length.

Finally, when I was satisfied that my appearance wouldn't cause suspicion, I exited the restroom and went to the ticket counter. I paid cash for a one-way ticket on the next bus that was leaving. It was going to a town that wasn't in the direction of my final destination, but I planned to change buses a couple of times to throw anyone who might come looking for me off the scent.

A few minutes later, a voice over the loudspeaker

announced that they were beginning to board. I handed the driver my ticket, took a window seat toward the back, and tried to calm my hammering nerves. I knew no one would be looking for me yet, but I also knew my heart wouldn't stop pounding until the bus had pulled away from the station and had passed the city limits. I thought back to the children, knew that by now they would have finished their ice cream and were probably horsing around and riding their uncharacteristic sugar high. By the time they began to get antsy, I would be gone, but they were obedient children and would not move from the parlor until the time to meet their father had come and gone. I assuaged my guilty conscience at leaving them by telling myself that Sarah was old enough to get the children back to the minivan and meet their father on her own.

The bus pulled backwards away from the curb, and I stared out the window, scanning the street for Isaiah and the children as we drove away and headed out of town. Sighing, I sank back into the surprisingly comfortable window seat I occupied and tried to take comfort in the peaceful rumble of the bus's tires under me. By the time I had been on the bus barely half an hour, the landscape was already beginning to change, a visual reminder that I really was leaving the only life I'd ever known behind. As I rode, I made plans for the next few hours in my head to calm myself. I made a mental note to buy a pair of scissors in the next town and cut my hair to a more reasonable length. I would also need to buy some food so that I wouldn't go hungry during the long hours on the bus.

Two o'clock arrived. Soon, I knew, the children would go find their father, and tell him that I hadn't come back from my errands. I got off in the next town and purchased another ticket for another bus, which luckily was leaving in only an hour. I resolved to be on it by the time Isaiah came looking for me. I got directions to a convenience store, where I purchased scissors, some food, and a map. As I waited for that bus to come, I borrowed a pen from the lady at the ticket counter and drew a circle around my destination.

Lupine, Colorado. The last known whereabouts of the only person in the world who could help me.

CHAPTER 2

Levi

"Let's ride!"

Grey Stone's call to the rest of the Stone Kings was met with loud hollers and whoops of affirmation. The brothers and I all straddled our bikes and started our engines. Grey, as president, moved to the front of the line, our road captain, Repo, beside him in the formation. Behind Grey was Trigger, the VP, and next to him the secretary, Winger. The rest of the officers fell in behind, two by two, then the other patched members, until it came to me. As Sergeant at Arms, I rode in the last row and to the right of the regular membership. We didn't have any new prospects at the moment, which meant that I was at the back of the formation.

It was a beautiful, cloudless Saturday morning. A few of the guys, myself included, were nursing hangovers from the night before, and I kept my dark glasses on against the glare of the sun. It was a perfect day for a ride, and if it had been one of many other Saturdays in late April, some or all of us would have been heading out to enjoy it the best way we knew how: with the wind in our hair and the engine rumbling beneath us.

But this was no ordinary Saturday. And this was no ordinary ride.

The Stone Kings were headed to Grand Junction, to form an honor guard for an Air Force member who had been killed in Afghanistan, and whose funeral was scheduled to be picketed by the Southbend Baptist Church.

Yeah, you've probably heard about the "church" I'm talking about. The one whose human excrement members hold up the "God hates fags" signs and show up at funerals and all sorts of other events with the goal of spreading their cancer far and wide. They say that our men and women in uniform dying is God's punishment to America for being a nation of sin and filth. Or some shit like that. "Divine retribution," they call it.

Picketing a goddamn service member's funeral.

Fuck that.

The Stone Kings MC, like a few other motorcycle clubs did from time to time around the country, was about to offer our services to protect the mourners and family from harassment from these pieces of shit. It was our job to make sure they wouldn't have to hear or see the disgusting things being said about their loved one. We were doing this at the request of one of the residents of Grand Junction, a neighbor of the deceased's family, who had been a friend of our club president's father growing up. The man had contacted Grey a couple of days ago out of the blue and asked whether the club could help out, and Grey had been only too happy to oblige.

What few details I knew of the dead serviceman's life had been told to us by Grey following his conversation with his dad's old friend. His name was Evan Kramer. He had been a young man, not even twenty-six yet, when he died. He had grown up the oldest of three children just outside of Grand

Junction, in a small town that didn't amount to much, barely meriting a dot on the map. Grey's contact said Evan had dreamed all his life of being in the military. At seventeen, he got accepted into the United States Air Force Academy in Colorado Springs, which was quite a feat. Free tuition to the Academy for all admitted students meant that a boy like him from a poor background had a chance to succeed that not many of his income level could afford. He had graduated with distinction from the Academy, and went on to serve as a commissioned officer for the Air Force. He did active duty in Afghanistan, and served two tours of duty before being killed in an indirect fire attack on Bagram Airfield. He was, by all accounts, a dedicated airman and an American hero.

It just so happened, he was also gay.

It was likely this last detail that had attracted the attention of Southbend Baptist.

And we were not about to let them fuck up this day for Evan Kramer's family.

As we rode the 120 or so odd miles from Lupine to Grand Junction, my idle mind drifted to the question of what makes some people evoke God's name as justification of their hatefulness and need to control others. It was a subject I'd thought about a lot over the years, partly as a result of personal experience. We all had dark sides of us, I knew. Hell, I'd be the first to admit that, living the life that I did. But I didn't need to use a leather-bound book to claim moral authority to do whatever the hell I damn well pleased. I wasn't that much of a fucking hypocrite.

In some ways, the very reason I had ended up the Sergeant at Arms in the Stone Kings MC was the direct result of the same kind of cancerous villainy we were on our way to protect the Kramer family from.

My name is Levi. My full name is Leviticus Josiah Wolff. I grew up in a religious fundamentalist cult called the Waiting For Zion Ranch.

WFZ is a community of the Fundamentalist Church of Jesus Christ of Latter-Day Saints. It's a polygamous sect that broke off from the main FLDS Church and left Utah in order to settle across the border in Arizona. They did this to get away from scrutiny by the feds, who were starting to crack down on polygamous practices in Utah.

I was born and raised in the WFZ community. I spent my entire life in that shithole, until I was seventeen and finally ran away, never to look back.

If you know much about the Bible, you know that Leviticus is the book about don'ts. It was written to tell the Israelites how God wanted them to act. This is the book my parents named me for. I'm sure the Southbend Baptist Church probably loved the hell out of Leviticus. They seemed like pretty hard-core Old Testament types. Leviticus has got all sorts of shit in it about sexual immorality, idolatry, and the like. The thing is, it also has stuff about not wearing clothing made of two kinds of material, and not eating shellfish or pork. Pretty sure at least a few Southbend members are gonna burn in hell if Leviticus is God's last word on living a holy life, 'cause I see a hell of a lot of stretchy polyester blends in that crowd.

Then there's my favorite Leviticus verse. Leviticus Chapter 19, Verse 28. I like it so much that I have a tattoo on my right shoulder that says, "Lev 19:28". It was the first one I ever got.

What's Leviticus 19:28, you ask?

"You shall not make any cuts in your body for the dead nor tattoo any marks upon you: I am the LORD."

King James Version.

My entire body, and all the ink on it, is one giant "fuck you" to all that hateful bullshit and everyone who uses the Old Testament as an excuse to hurt and judge other people.

If there is a God out there, I can't believe He would waste His time trying to police whether we ate shrimp, or whether someone has ink. And any God worth believing in would never condone what the Southbend Baptist Church does in His name. A God who would require that of His followers is no God I could ever believe in.

As I rode with my brothers to protect the family of a man who had died for our country, I thought about the so-called "family" I had left behind at the WFZ Ranch all those years ago. To my actual family and everyone else I had grown up around, I was good as dead, I knew. I was shunned, and my name would never be mentioned again by my parents or my siblings. For them, it was as though I had never existed.

And no one who knew me now as Levi Wolff, Sergeant at Arms of the Stone Kings MC knew my background, where I came from or what I left behind. And that's the way I liked it. No past, no future. Only the present. No one's laws but my own to uphold. And the laws of my club.

We arrived in Grand Junction about two hours before the funeral was supposed to start, to make sure we got there before the Southbend people did. St. Mark's Catholic Church was on the north side of town, a small church in a style I didn't know the name for but that made me think of Mexico, like a lot of architecture in the area. Another chapter of the Stone Kings club, from Las Cruces, was there to meet us, too. Grey greeted the chapter president, whose name was Slayer, and the two of them took off to meet with their contact. A few minutes later, they came back, and Grey clapped a hand on Slayer's shoulder before they separated to go over the plan with their prospective clubs.

Grey came over to the parking lot across the street from the church where we had parked our bikes. "Slayer's guys are going to set up a perimeter around the church in case any stray assholes decide to try to get too close or go inside," he said, nodding back toward the church. "We're gonna push back the protesters, make a wall of ourselves to make sure they don't get close enough for the mourners to hear or see them. Rev our engines to drown out what they say, so no one has to listen to their bullshit. After the funeral, we'll ride behind the procession to the cemetery and mount a guard there."

I nodded and turned to Trig and Repo. "Sounds good. Let's not let these demented fucks soil this service member's final goodbye."

We set up the perimeter and the blockade. Not long after cars began to arrive filled with downcast people in dark, somber clothing, a group of six middle-aged men with signs approached and began to walk toward the church. When they were about twenty feet away from us, Trigger yelled out, "That's close enough. Stay right where you are."

One of the men, who held a sign that said, "Pray for more dead soldiers," made a move as though he intended to come closer, but one step forward by Trigger stopped him. "I said, that's as far as you're going," Trigger said calmly, but there was an unmistakable warning in his voice that conveyed that he expected to be obeyed.

"Or what?" the man sneered. "How you gonna stop us? You ain't the cops."

I had never wanted to hit a man so badly before,

and I had hit plenty of people. I could imagine the satisfying crunch it would make when his teeth broke under my fist. Barely resisting the impulse, I walked forward until I was mere inches from the man. I had at least six inches on him, and though he probably weighed in at ten to twenty more pounds than I did, most of his weight was in the considerable paunch hanging over his belt. I saw his eyes widen as they went to the tattoos that went up and down my arms. I leaned in just enough so that I towered over him slightly.

"Most of us have been to prison at one point or another," I said through clenched teeth. "In the majority of cases, it was for assault. On the off chance that the cops don't send us all fruit baskets for beating the life out of you bunch of miserable shits, I think I'm speaking for all my brothers when I say we would be more than happy to take the risk of getting arrested for stopping you from going any closer."

The fat sign-holder blanched. He threw a nervous glance at his buddies and stepped back far enough to try and gain back a little of his dignity. "I sure as hell ain't gonna waste my time on a bunch of biker thugs," he spat out. I could feel my right hand curl into a fist, but stayed where I was. As much as I wanted to escalate this, our duty was to the dead serviceman and his family right now, and that meant keeping the peace if at all possible.

The sign-bearers moved into a shitty little cluster and talked among themselves, and a few more people began to arrive with signs of their own, until there were about twenty people there to picket, including one child, a little boy of no more than eight years old. He held a sign that said, "God bless 9/11." I felt my gorge rise in disgust that anyone could teach such hate to such a small child. The boy looked like he hardly knew what was going on. I couldn't help but think of myself at that age, and how confusing I must have found the world and what those around me said about how it worked.

The picketers tried their best to disrupt things, but there were a hell of a lot more of us than there were of them, and they seemed pretty intimidated by our considerable presence. They tried to start chants from time to time, and one of them even had a bullhorn, but every time they'd start making noise, a few of the brothers would rev their engines so loud it was impossible to hear anything they were saying. After a while the bullhorn guy, a scrawny meth-head looking guy with wild eyes and shitty teeth, was the only one shouting anymore, and so Repo just kept his engine revved up until the guy got hoarse and eventually gave up trying to yell.

After the funeral was over, we got back in formation and followed the funeral procession out to the cemetery. Someone had figured out to bring a bunch of American flags, and each of us fixed them to the backs of our bikes to fly behind us as we rode to the grave site. Just in case, we posted men at all the entrances to the cemetery and mounted a perimeter around the graveside service, but I guessed the Southbend Baptist fucks had gotten tired of being drowned out, because they didn't show up. I watched from a distance as a rank of Air Force servicemen marched to the back of the hearse to serve as pallbearers for the young man they were about to bury. I watched as they carried him to his grave site, and as they folded the flag that covered the casket and presented it to a woman who had to be Evan Kramer's mother. I listened as the priest murmured some words and prayers of comfort to the bereaved. And finally, I watched as the casket was lowered into the ground, with the friends and family watching in silence.

A few people stepped forward and placed flowers either next to the site, or tossed a single rose in on top of the casket. A man whom I figured to be

Evan's father took his mother by the elbow and led her away as she sobbed quietly. A teenage boy and a slightly younger girl trailed behind them, looking shell-shocked. I took a deep breath and let it out, a wave of sadness washing over me. A young life was gone, leaving pain and emptiness in its wake.

As people made their way from the graveside, Evan's parents walked toward us, coming to a stop in front of Trigger and me. The woman lifted the veil she was wearing to look at us. She was pretty, despite her pallor and the expression of pain etched in her features. "Thank you," she whispered, her lip trembling. "Thank you."

"Ma'am," Trigger nodded. "Sir. It was an honor."

They turned away, then, and we watched the friends and family of Evan Kramer slowly walk back to their cars. They were mostly silent, except for an occasional low remark from one to another. From here, they would probably be going back to the church basement, to push around food on their plates that members of their congregation had prepared for them. Or maybe they'd gather at the Kramers' house, where well-wishers would bring them casseroles and take care of cleaning up afterwards. I watched the cars drive away, one after the other, a solemn cortege. As terrible as it was that Evan Kramer had to die, I was glad that he had family to grieve for him.

The ride back to Lupine gave me far too much time alone with my thoughts, and by the time we got to the clubhouse, the whole damn thing had me surly and out of sorts. I didn't seem to be the only one. The brothers stepped off their bikes one by one, and headed inside almost as quietly as the funeral procession had left.

A few of the men headed to the clubhouse bar to unwind after the somber afternoon. "Jesus," Winger, our secretary, swore as he went back behind the bar and popped the top off a bottle of beer. "After all that, I need booze and pussy."

He took a long swig, then headed off to find one of the willing women who made it a habit of hanging around the club. I knew he wouldn't need to look very far. I also knew instinctively that tonight would be a night of heavy drinking and partying, to stave off the demons we had all glimpsed today. Myself included.

CHAPTER 3

Cherish

It took me three days to get to Lupine, Colorado. Three days of getting off of one bus, waiting hours for the next one to arrive, and living in a more or less constant state of panic that someone from the WFZ Ranch would find me and drag me back home. I knew that the leader, Harlan Radleff, would never let me go without attempting to find me and drag me back. It had happened before. People who left and never came back were bad for the interior harmony of the community. The idea that anyone would want to leave that earthly paradise would send whispers and rumors skittering around the Ranch, and Radleff and his men wanted to avoid that whenever possible. I just had to hope that the precautions I had taken to avoid being followed would be enough to keep them from figuring out where I was until eventually they just gave up.

Only a handful of people had ever tried to leave in my memory, and when, inevitably, they were brought back, they were kept in isolation for a few days, far from curious eyes. When they finally rejoined the community again, they usually said that they had fallen ill from some malady they had picked up outside the Ranch and had to be nursed back to health. Their drawn expressions and tired eyes seemed to corroborate that explanation, but I think many knew better.

Usually, once someone had tried to leave and failed, they didn't try again. In fact, I could only remember one person ever getting out successfully and not returning. That person was who I had come so far to find.

I had been wearing the same set of clothes since my escape, and hadn't been able to bathe except by wiping myself off with wet paper towels in bus terminal restrooms. I had almost run out of the money I'd managed to bring, even as careful as I had been with it, and I was exhausted from the little bits of fitful sleep I had managed on the road, having been too afraid of discovery to let myself nap in bus stations.

On the morning I finally got to Lupine, I used most of my remaining money treating myself to a real breakfast in a diner to fortify myself, and then spent the next few hours making inquiries about the person I had come to see. Mistakenly, I had thought that once I was in Lupine, the hard part would be over. It turned out that tracking him down was more difficult than I imagined it would be.

In fairness, I didn't know what I had expected. All the information I had — the sum total of all the things I had heard about him since he had disappeared — was his name and the name of the town he was said to have gone to. And that he was a biker. Not like a bicyclist. A motorcycle rider. And to hear my brother tell it, he was probably a rapist and an axe murderer to boot.

Which raised the question of why in heaven's name I was trying to find him in the first place.

The truth was, I didn't see that I had much

choice. Maybe other people in the world were just stronger than I was. It had taken me more than a year to finally convince myself that I had to leave the Ranch — that any life on the outside would be better than the life I was condemned to there. I had spent months of planning, secreting away clothes and money that I would need to get away and start fresh somewhere else. I had spent countless nights lying awake, practically paralyzed with fear that Isaiah would find where I had hidden those things and beat me, then haul me in front of the leader and the council for my punishment. After all of that, I had somehow found the courage to actually leave. But the only way I was able to manage to convince myself to actually go through with it was by telling myself that there was someone out there on the other side who would help me. Who *had* to help me. Even if he didn't want to. Simply because he was the only one who could.

At the restaurant where I bought juice, eggs, and hash browns, I asked the waitress if she knew a man named Leviticus. She looked at me like I had two heads. "Leviticus?" the waitress squeaked, as though I'd said his name was Daffy Duck. "No, sorry, I don't know anyone with a name like that."

My face flushed in embarrassment. I was

becoming more or less used to feeling like a space alien in my interactions the past few days. I had thought that changing my clothing would be enough to help me pass as one of the "worldly" people (as the people in the community called them), but it seemed as though the things that came out of my mouth were just as strange. I didn't *think* it was my appearance that was calling attention to me. Though my clothes were a little dirty by now, they didn't seem too different from what other people were wearing around me, though perhaps a little less revealing than the clothing preferred by most of the young women my age.

I had finally managed to cut my hair in a gas station bathroom when one of the buses I was on stopped for a break. It had never been cut in my lifetime, as women of the WFZ Ranch were told that to cut their hair was a sin in the eyes of God. My hands were shaking as I picked up the scissors to do something that no woman in the community would ever think of doing. In the end, I had been too chicken to do anything drastic, but I did manage to cut off almost a foot, and it now fell to the middle of my back, which seemed like a "normal" length that wouldn't attract attention. I had bought a toothbrush and toothpaste at the same stop, so I didn't think my oral hygiene was causing any negative reactions.

I tried again with the waitress. "Well, would you know where I could find a biker? Like, a motorcycle rider?"

If anything, the question just seemed to amuse her more. "Like, *any* motorcycle rider?" she asked, her darkly penciled brow cocking in what I was pretty sure was mockery.

"The person I'm looking for is a motorcycle rider," I explained, willing the ever-hotter flush in my cheeks to go away. "I thought, if I could find someone who knew other motorcycle riders, they might be able to tell me where he is."

She shrugged. "You could just go hang out downtown and wait for someone on a motorcycle to show up," she suggested. Her eyes flicked away from me toward a table of boys about her age who were roughhousing noisily. It was clear she was getting bored with talking to me. I thanked her, and she wasted no time setting down my check and heading toward the boys' table. I absently watched her as she flirted shamelessly with the best-looking of them, her voice growing teasing and animated.

Taking a sip of my orange juice, I thought about my next move. Actually, the waitress's suggestion about going downtown and trying to find a motorcycle rider wasn't a bad one. At any rate, I couldn't be very choosy, considering I had basically no other ideas. I reached into my pocket for my few remaining bills, paid my tab, and wandered outside.

Downtown Lupine was about a mile and a half from where the bus had dropped me off at a combination bus depot and truck stop. I walked the distance along a dusty highway with no sidewalks, and eventually came across the area, which primarily consisted of one long main street lined with bars, restaurants, and shops of various kinds. I covered the several blocks from one end to the other, noting a smattering of motorcycles along the way. Eventually, I stopped in front of another diner, where a cluster of them were parked. These machines were larger and more imposing than the others I had seen, and some of them had leather side bags, or skull designs on the gas tank. Pushing down my nervousness, I decided that talking to whoever owned these motorcycles would probably be my best shot at learning where Leviticus was. There were no benches or places to sit that I could see, so I sat down awkwardly on the curb to wait.

I'm not sure how much time passed, but eventually a group of men came out of the diner talking in loud voices. They were wearing jeans and leather vests with patches on them that said undecipherable things like "Road Capt." and "Enforcer" and a couple of them had long, thick beards. Tattoos lined their muscled arms, and one of them immediately lit up a cigarette as soon as they were outside.

I stood up, brushed off the backside of my jeans and took a deep breath. "Excuse me," I called out to them.

The one with the longest beard turned to look at me, smiling to reveal a set of straight, very white teeth. He reminded me of the big bad wolf in the fairy tale we read to children at the Ranch. "Well, well, well, darlin', what can we do for you?" he said in a voice that was both a challenge and an invitation.

I took a few steps forward and tried to keep my voice from trembling. "I'm looking for someone. A motor... a biker. And I was wondering if you might know where he is. "

Beard looked at another of the men, with razored hair about the same length as his whiskers. "If you're lookin' for a man, darlin', I can help you out," he leered suggestively.

A wave of fright shot through me. Suddenly, I realized this might not be such a good idea. Nervously, I looked around, reassured that there were a few other people on the street who would hear me if I cried out. "I'm sorry, no," I replied in a shaking voice. I didn't want to provoke these dangerous men in any way. "It's a particular person I'm looking for. His name is Leviticus Wolff."

"Leviticus Wolff?" Beard repeated in disbelief. His tone matched the one the waitress had used when I'd said Leviticus's name, and I almost laughed at how similar this enormous bearded man sounded to the teenage girl. He laughed then, a loud bark, and turned to his friends. "Levi's name is fuckin' *Leviticus?*"

I flinched at the curse, but otherwise didn't react as the men burst into loud laughter. Nonetheless, my heart leapt at what he had said. They knew Leviticus! But apparently he went by Levi now. I made a mental note of it; the fact that these men didn't know his full name might mean that he didn't want them to, for some reason.

I waited until their laughter had died down and repeated my question. "Do you know where Levit… where Levi is?"

"Honey, you sure you know what you're gettin' into here?" a man whose head was shaved clean spoke up. His eyes raked slowly over me, lingering on my breasts, making me feel as though I was naked instead of wearing a loose-fitting T-shirt.

"He's… He's someone I know from way back," I lied. "I have a message for him." I hadn't though through this part of my plan very well, I realized. I should have thought of some plausible reason why a dangerous biker would want to talk to me.

"You got a message for him?" Shaved Head mocked. "This the pony express or something? Why the fuck don't you just call him?"

"I don't have his phone number," I explained. *Or a cell phone.*

"Look, darlin'," Beard began. He shook his head slightly. "You need to get in touch with Levi, you're just gonna have to figure out how to do that yourself. I don't know what your business is with him, but you look like a nice enough girl. Why don't you run along, find yourself a nice college student or male librarian or something." He nodded once toward the man beside him. "Come on, let's go."

"You have a nice day, now," Shaved Head

drawled, winking at me so suggestively it made my cheeks burn hot. The men walked past me and headed toward their bikes, a couple of them murmuring crudely about how I would look naked just loudly enough for me to hear them. As I watched them go, I noticed that the patches on the backs of their vests all said the same thing: Stone Kings MC.

I watched them pull away, then sat back down on the curb to think. The encounter with the bikers had left me shaken and rethinking my plans. I had thought I'd prepared myself for the possibility that Leviticus was in some sort of motorcycle gang, and that it might be dangerous to go see him, but the reality had been much more frightening than I had expected. Still, I was out of money and out of ideas, and being all alone with no one to help me and nowhere to stay was just as frightening. I had to believe that even if Leviticus was a hardened criminal, he would at least take pity on me and give me a few dollars or point me toward someone who could. Surely he would help someone who had escaped our community like he had? Of course, he had been gone for years — more than ten, at least. I didn't even really know him when I was a child, and I had absolutely no idea the kind of man he'd become. There was always the possibility that he had no trace left of any morals or decency. He belonged to a motorcycle gang, after all. What if I found him, and instead of helping me, he... did to me what the men who were his friends had made it clear that they wanted to do, with their leering and suggestive words?

I shuddered, and almost started crying at the sudden realization of how alone I really was and how much potential danger I was in. Growing up in the faith, in the center of a tight-knit and isolated community, I had never been alone before. Family and friends were constantly around me. In fact, at the Ranch, I hardly ever had a moment to myself, unless I was taking care of my bodily functions or getting dressed or undressed. By contrast, in the three days I had been gone, I had spoken to no one apart from the impersonal few words necessary to order food or buy something at a store. The singularity of my purpose — to get to Lupine, to make contact with the only person I had any connection to in the outside world — had mostly kept me from considering how alone I truly was. But now, I was lonely, scared, and facing the very real possibility that at best, Leviticus Wolff would be completely indifferent to me. And at worst...

A slight sob escaped me. An older man passing

by me turned at the sound to look at me curiously. I cleared my throat and gave him what I hoped was a reassuring smile. I stood up abruptly before he could ask me anything, and started walking purposefully in the other direction as though I had suddenly remembered an appointment. *Stop it, Cherish,* I told myself sternly. No matter what happened, I scolded myself, it would be better than what I had left. Here I was, wringing my hands at the thought that some dangerous biker might take my virtue. Was that really any worse than what had already happened to me?

It was a sad realization that a total stranger forcing himself upon me was really not much worse than what I already went through on a daily basis back home. I was not innocent to the ways and dangers of a man's desire, having been married not once, but twice before. My first husband, Abram Radleff, had been the brother of our leader, Harlan Radleff. I was Abram's his fourth and final wife, the other three having died, the last of cancer. I had been only sixteen at the time of our marriage. Thankfully, Abram, at almost eighty, was too old and frail to consummate the marriage, so I was spared being deflowered by him.

After Abram died, I was married off to Isaiah, at

nineteen. Isaiah, at forty-five years old, had one wife before me, Carolyn, whose bed he rarely seemed to share after our marriage.

The night of our wedding, despite my terror, I did my wifely duty and lay still as I had been told to do, while he took his pleasure with me. Despite the shock of searing pain, I made sure not to cry out when he first entered me. The next night, and every night after that, he made clear that he expected me to get into bed and wait for him, and I did so, listening with revulsion to his animal pants and groans and trying not to smell his stagnant breath as he thrashed and thrust inside me. Once, I had been taken ill with a fever, and was so tired and achy that I tried to tell him no. When he pushed me back on the bed and tried to take me by force, I tried to fight him, even though I was weak from the sickness. Before I realized what was happening, he had raised his arm and backhanded me across the face, splitting my bottom lip open with the force of it. After that, I never dared fight him again.

Whatever awaited me now, I reminded myself bitterly, short of death it could only be as bad as what was waiting for me back at the Ranch. I swore to myself for the hundredth time that I would never go back, no matter what.

I spent the afternoon walking up and down Main Street in Lupine, asking random strangers if they knew where the Stone Kings MC could be found. Many of them looked at me with surprise and warned me against what I was asking. Finally, a young man of about my age told me that they had a clubhouse at the edge of town, and explained to me where it was. He stared after me curiously as I thanked him and set off on foot. I had no idea how far I would have to walk to get there, but it didn't matter as I had no other option but to walk.

Eventually, I came to a large, two-story structure that looked a bit like a small warehouse or commercial building. About twenty motorcycles were parked in two long rows in the parking lot. It was as though someone had dumped a bucket of ice in my stomach: this was it. For better or for worse, I had finally reached the end of my journey.

After all I had done to get here, I couldn't make myself take the final steps and go inside the building. I knew I would feel safer outside meeting Levi, even if, unlike downtown, no one was around to hear me if anything happened. Fortunately, I didn't have to wait very long before a tall, thin man with short red hair and a beard came out and started toward the far row of motorcycles. I approached him, asked if he would tell Levi Wolff I was there to see him, and sat down at an ancient, peeling picnic table outside the entrance to wait.

CHAPTER 4

Levi

I had just managed to kick Trigger's ass in an arm wrestling match and was basking in the glory of him having to serve me up a shot like a little bitch, when Pig came up next to me at the bar.

"Levi, there's some chick in a Minions shirt outside to see you."

"What the fuck?" I cocked a brow at him. "What did you say?"

"Some chick in a Minions T-shirt. She's waiting outside."

I shook my head and frowned, trying to get my head around what the hell he was talking about. The only chicks I knew wore leather and skin-tight Harley tanks, not some fuckin' cartoon character shirt. My mind's eye conjured up an image of a twelve year-old girl, but no twelve year-old was gonna be waiting outside a biker clubhouse unless she was serious jail bait.

"You're shitting me." I said, frowning. "She say what she want?"

"Nope," Pig replied, taking a stool next to me and reaching for the Jack.

I was half-inclined just to ignore whoever it was and give Trig the rematch he was begging for, but curiosity got the better of me. Standing up, I reached my arms behind my head and stretched, then wandered outside, trying to think of any civilian chick that could possibly be stupid or brave enough to come by the MC to find me.

The sun was bright and I didn't have my shades on me, so at first all I could see was a fucking ridiculous yellow shirt with one of those damn googly-eyed things on it, sitting on our picnic table. I walked toward it, squinting, my hand raised to shade my eyes. "You wanted to talk to me?" I asked the figure.

"Leviticus?" she said in a questioning voice, and stood up.

What. The. Fuck.

I stopped dead in my tracks as soon as I heard the name that no one had called me for a dozen years. My fists clenched involuntarily as my eyes finally began to adjust to the glaring sunlight enough for me to see who the voice belonged to. She looked to be in her early twenties, though she wasn't wearing any makeup. Most twenty-something women I knew wouldn't be caught dead in public without it. That fucking ridiculous yellow shirt obscured whatever figure she might be hiding under it, and made her look even younger. She was wearing jeans and dusty flip flops. Her arms hung awkwardly at her sides, though the longer I stared at her without speaking, she crossed them in front of her self-consciously, as though to defend herself. Dark reddish-brown hair fell down past her shoulders to the middle of her back, and framed her heart-shaped face in gentle, artless waves. Her eyes were dark and wide as she stared at me, her plump lips slightly parted in an expression I couldn't quite read, but that was probably fear.

Good. I wanted her to be scared. Whoever she was, she had no business here.

Leviticus, she had called me. That took care of one of my questions. There was only one place she could be from.

My past.

"It's Levi," I barked back at her. It came out more harshly than I had meant to, but I told myself I didn't care.

She shrank back for a moment, and looked down. "I'm sorry. Levi," she mumbled.

"What the fuck do you want?" I snarled at her. She looked so nervous that I felt just a little bit bad about the way I was talking to her, but too fucking bad. I didn't want her here. Whatever the fuck she was trying to pull, the quickest way to get her gone was to show her that she was not welcome, in no uncertain terms. The man she was looking for didn't exist anymore. There was no reason for her to be here. None.

"It's just… I…" she began. Her eyes filled with sudden tears, and she brushed at them distractedly with the back of one hand. "I'm sorry," she stammered. "I guess I didn't really plan this part out very well."

"What part?" I demanded. "You shouldn't be here." *I know where you're from, little girl. You need to go back there right now, before someone gets hurt.*

"I'm…" she took a deep breath, and let it out slowly. When she started again, her voice was more or less steady. "My name is Cherish Holmes," she said, looking me directly in the eye. "I'm from the Waiting For Zion Ranch." Her eyes flickered for a moment. "At least, I was. I've run away. I left the Ranch." Her jaw set, and she continued. "I'm hoping you'll help me."

"Help you?" I asked incredulously, scoffing. "How the hell can I help you? Do you even know where you are?"

"Lupine, Colorado, at the clubhouse of the Stone Kings Motorcycle Gang," she answered. Her chin jutted almost defiantly.

In spite of myself, I had to laugh. "It's a club, not a gang," I said, one corner of my mouth curving upward.

"Club, then," she corrected, her face coloring. "I know you're a member of the club. And I know you used to be in the WFZ community, too."

My anger surged back. "How the hell do you know about me?" I demanded, taking a threatening step closer. This was already too much information for her to have. I needed to get her the hell away from here. The last thing I needed was some ex-cult member hanging on to me, expecting me to help her make it in the cold, cruel world. I was not a babysitter for a young, beautiful woman who had no fucking experience with life outside her sheltered little existence. I had barely made it out myself, and I was the worse for wear in every respect.

"My brother is Elias Holmes. You were friends when you were kids."

My mind flashed back to my childhood. *Elias.* The image of a freckled redhead with a gap-toothed grin came to my mind. The two of us used to play together during the rare times where there was any room for recreation between school, chores, and prayer. I remember that Elias's mother hadn't liked me much, and thought I was a bad influence on her son. I laughed to myself at the memory. *She was a perceptive woman.*

The girl, Cherish, widened her eyes a bit at my sudden laugh. "You remember him, don't you?" she asked. "I'm not lying, I swear."

I shook my head and snorted. "I know you're not lying," I scowled at her. "I remember your brother. Besides, you look like the last person in the world who would be capable of telling a lie."

To my amusement, she seemed actually put out by that remark. "I can so tell a lie." She jutted her chin at me defiantly. "I had to conceal my escape plans from everybody, for months."

"Oh yeah?" I asked mockingly, but curious in spite of myself. "Who'd you have to hide from?"

"My husband," she retorted. "My stepchildren."

Her voice tripped over the words, and strangely, my stomach dropped to hear them. To imagine her married, when she couldn't be more than twenty-one or twenty-two… well, it's not that she wasn't old enough. Hell, twenty-two was practically ancient for a woman to be unmarried in the WFZ. But she just seemed so… innocent. Granted, the women I was used to being around these days looked older at eighteen than this one probably would at thirty. But still. Given what I knew about the place she had escaped, I could fill in some of the blanks of what her marriage had probably been like. And it wasn't pretty.

"Wait a minute," I said, my mind fixing on something she had said. "You said your name was Cherish Holmes. But if you're married…"

She nodded. "My married name is Whitehead." Her jaw set. "*Was* Whitehead," she corrected.

I dimly remembered the name. "Which Whitehead?" I asked.

"Isaiah," she murmured. Her eyes grew dark, troubled, and a pang of sympathy shot through me. The Whiteheads were one of the most prominent families of the WFZ, second only to the Radleffs. Isaiah Whitehead, if I remembered correctly, had been a brooding, borderline sadistic asshole, the kind of bully that cults like the WFZ bred like rabbits. Their version of God's will somehow seemed to always coincidentally line up with whatever the hell they wanted to do, anyway. Isaiah Whitehead had been about thirty or so when I left the faith. As I gazed at Cherish now, my stomach twisted at the thought of him bedding her, my fist clenching involuntarily at the idea of her forced to do her wifely duty by him.

Women didn't have the right to say no in the WFZ community. Their primary duty was to be entirely subservient to their husbands in all things. Judging from the fact that Cherish had chosen to run rather than stay with her husband told me I probably had a pretty accurate picture of what her marriage had been like.

"Stepkids, you said?" I asked, noting that she hadn't mentioned children.

"Yes," she nodded. "Isaiah and I did not have the… did not have children of our own." Her face colored again at the reference to sex. Sudden anger flooded through me at the realization that she had probably never experienced it as anything but pain or unpleasant duty. I didn't know why I cared, exactly, but it galled me that she had probably only experienced sex as pain and unpleasant obligation.

Yes you do, an inner voice said. *You know exactly why it pisses you off.*

Fuck. That fucking cult. I had tried so hard to get away from it and never think of that god-forsaken place again. It made me furious to have to think of that band of sick assholes again.

Suddenly, my mind registered something else Cherish had said. "Wait," I said. "You said your brother told you where I was?" How the hell did Elias know anything about me? And had he helped Cherish to escape?

"No," she shook her head. "He didn't tell me. Not exactly." She sighed as she ran a hand through her hair and sat back down on the picnic table. For the first time, I realized how exhausted she probably was, and how hard it must have been for her to get here, with no car and no resources.

"Elias somehow heard through the grapevine that you had come here," she continued tiredly. "You're the only person I can remember who ever left and didn't come back. You're shunned, you know. Your name isn't to be spoken by anyone. Not even your family." She looked up suddenly, embarrassed. "I'm sorry. I'm sure that isn't easy to hear."

"No skin off my nose," I snorted. I had said goodbye to my family a long time ago.

"Anyway," she went on, "that doesn't keep people from gossiping, of course. Whispering.

You're like this… this boogey man in people's minds. You're the fallen one who has gone to the Devil. They know that you left for a place called Lupine, which they say is the symbol of the devil because it's named after a wolf, and that you're a killer in a motorcycle gang."

I burst into laughter. "Lupine isn't named after a wolf, it's named after a goddamn flower."

"Well, anyway," she shrugged. "That's what they say."

My laughter subsided, and I tilted my head at her in confusion. "So, you heard I lived in a town named after Satan, and that I'm a killer, and you decided that it would be a good idea to come find me?" I smirked.

She looked up at me, her dark eyes clear and frank. "I had to get out. You were the only person I knew who might help me."

Shit. That wasn't where I wanted this to go. I had been trying to get rid of her, but I had gotten distracted by her story in spite of myself.

"Look," I said, shaking my head. "I can't help you. I'm not exactly what Elias told you I was, but

I'm not that far off. My life doesn't have any room in it for helping out some woman I've never met. I can't do anything for you."

A look of desperation and fear crossed her face. She stood up from the picnic table and took a few steps forward, until she was facing me not two feet away. Her large, dark eyes met mine, imploring me without words, and a shock of electricity shot through me before I knew what was happening. Up until now, I had noticed that she was pretty, but the fucking Minions shirt she was wearing had been so distracting that I hadn't paid much more attention than that. Up close, with her face raised toward me, I realized for the first time that she was fucking beautiful. Her creamy, clear skin set off the full, pouty pinkness of her lips, and before I realized what was going on, I had grown hard as a rock as I my mind conjured up an image of how that soft, full mouth would look wrapped around my dick.

"Please," she said simply as I fought for self-control. She didn't seem to have any idea the fucking effect she was having on me as her voice lowered to a whisper. "'I don't have any place else to go. I don't have any money left." Her eyes searched mine, begging me, and my cock jumped in my pants. "Please," she repeated, softer this time. "Please, just help me find someplace to sleep tonight, and take a shower. I promise I'll leave you alone after that."

Goddamn. My heart was slamming against my ribcage so hard I was afraid she'd hear it. She couldn't have known that all I could think of now was joining her naked body in the shower she'd just asked for, and hearing that throaty little voice beg me for something else entirely. I took a step back and arranged my face in an angry frown. *Fuck.*

I couldn't believe I was about to do this. Grey would probably fucking kill me for it.

"Okay," I growled at her. "One night. One night only." I nodded back toward the clubhouse. "There's an apartment upstairs. You can stay there. It's got a bathroom with a shower." *And a lock on the door.*

"Oh, thank you!" she cried, jumping up and down slightly. She smiled at me then, a bright, dazzling smile that lit up her whole face and made my heart start slamming in my chest again. "Thank you so much, Levi!" She stepped forward just a little, then pulled back in embarrassment, her arms clasped tightly to her chest.

Grumbling to myself, I had her follow me to the

entrance to the clubhouse and held the door open for her. Inside, I led her through the bar, upstairs, to the nicest of the apartments we kept. After telling her as quickly as I could where things were and, I got the hell out of there and went back downstairs. I announced to the astonished men who had watched me lead her in that she was staying for one night, and that she was strictly off limits.

Then I took out my cell and called the only person I could think of to come help me the fuck out.

"Hey, Seton?" I said when she answered. "I've got a situation."

CHAPTER 5

Cherish

I don't know what I had expected when I met Levi, but the reality of him was both exactly right and not even close.

I had had only the very vaguest memory of him from when I was a child. After all, he had left when I was probably no more than seven or eight years old. When I started making my plans to escape the WFZ Ranch, I hadn't let myself think too much about what might be awaiting me in Lupine. When Elias said that Leviticus had joined a motorcycle gang ("*club*," I reminded myself now), I had imagined a big, hulking bald man with a long, menacing beard, wearing leather and covered in tattoos.

Well, I had gotten the tattoos right. Almost every surface of his skin below his neck seemed to be covered with them. (In spite of myself, my mind wandered to whether he was tattooed *everywhere*, and I blushed furiously at the thought.) And I had the beard right, as well, though it was shorter and lighter than I had expected, a slightly more reddish tint than the reddish-brown of his hair.

What I hadn't gotten right was how… attractive he was. Masculine, in a way that was both dangerous and thrilling. Somehow the tattoos, which I had imagined as scary, were actually sort of beautiful. The colorful, geometric patterns accentuated the chiseled muscles on his arms. Tattoos were strictly forbidden in the faith, as were any body alterations, and I had never really seen any up close before. The ones Levi had made my eyes want to linger on his body, and even to touch his skin, to see whether it felt any different on the parts that were covered with the designs.

I hadn't gotten his eyes right, either. I half-expected them to be dark, menacing, mean. Instead, they were green, a light, penetrating color that was so mesmerizing that I had to work not to fixate on them.

Leviticus had been furious to see me. I hadn't allowed myself to consider that he might be, but I couldn't blame him for it. After all, here I was, dropping unannounced into his life from a world he had risked everything to leave behind. I had been lucky, I knew, that he had agreed to help me at all. And frankly, I had been lucky that he wasn't the evil demon that the community made him out to be. He was scary, for sure. But I sensed that his intention was not to hurt me. He just wanted me gone. It fairly radiated off of him when he looked at me. And I had to live with that, and accept it. It was his right to be angry with me for disrupting his life.

Levi led me through the bar of the clubhouse, the eyes of several other tattooed men and a few busty, made-up women following us curiously. We went up a flight of stairs to the second floor. The doors to most of the rooms were closed, but he led me to one at the far end of a hall and opened it without a key.

"Here," he said gruffly. "Bed's over there, bathroom's through there. Make yourself comfortable. I'm gonna call my president's old lady to check in on you in a little while. Lock the door."

And with that, he was gone.

I looked around the sparsely furnished apartment, then sank down on the bed. It was surprisingly comfortable, or maybe it was just that I was exhausted. I took a deep breath and let it out slowly. For the first time in almost four days, I was safe, at least momentarily. I didn't have to look over my shoulder every second. Levi had told me I could only stay for only one night, but I couldn't let myself think about that now. I knew I needed to just focus on the moment at hand, or otherwise I'd go crazy with fear and worry. Tomorrow was tomorrow. I'd think about what to do then.

I resisted the temptation to just lie back and close my eyes, knowing that I'd be asleep in a heartbeat. Instead, I kicked off my flip flops, spent a few moments massaging my dirty, aching feet, and went into the bathroom. I turned on the shower as hot as I could stand it, and stood under the water for close to twenty minutes, luxuriating in the pleasure of the spray beating against my skin. I had never taken such a long shower before, but I couldn't seem to get myself to shut the water off. I had brought a couple of travel bottles of shampoo with me, and I used an entire small bottle on my hair, breathing in the scent and being thankful for this smallest of pleasures.

Once I was out of the shower, I stood on the mat with a bath towel around me and fretted at the realization that I'd have to put my dirty clothes back on. Unfortunately, I had no choice. I had brought a few spare pairs of underwear, though, so it wasn't as bad as it could have been. I carefully washed the underwear I had been wearing in the sink and hung it up in the shower to dry. I towel dried my hair, running my hands through it like a comb, then went back out to the main room, where I lay back down on the bed and, as I knew I would, promptly fell asleep.

A discreet knock on the door woke me up some time later, jarring me out of a confused dream full of tattooed men and the noise of tires on highways. I rose groggily and flipped the deadbolt on the door. A young woman stood on the other side, a paper shopping bag in her arms.

"Hi, I'm Seton," she said, smiling. "You must be Cherish. Can I come in?"

I stood back from the door and she strode in and set the shopping bag on the table in the kitchenette. When Levi had mentioned something about an old lady, I expected a grandmotherly type, or at least someone my mother's age. Seton looked to be about twenty-five or so, and she was exceptionally pretty, with wavy brown hair and flashing green eyes. She was dressed simply but stylishly in a red top and jeans that hugged her body attractively.

"Levi called me and asked me to come help you out. He said you needed a change of clothes." She turned toward me now, eyeing the dirty T-shirt I had had no choice but to put back on after my shower. Her mouth twitched up at the corners. "He wasn't kidding."

I opened my mouth to ask what she meant, but her eyes told me everything I needed to know. "I didn't have many choices at the Goodwill," I said, looking down at the shirt. "Not good?"

"Not good," she agreed cheerfully. "Here, give me that, and I can wash it. I'll give it back, but only if you promise you'll only use it for sleeping."

I flushed with embarrassment as I realized how ridiculous I must look, but I could tell she wasn't trying to be mean to me. I swallowed my pride and forced myself to smile. "Thank you," I nodded.

Her hand was still out, and I suddenly realized

she meant for me to take my shirt off right there and give it to her. My eyes darted toward the bathroom, and Seton must have realized I wasn't comfortable undressing in front of a stranger. "Here," she said gently, picking up the shopping bag and handing it to me. "There should be some things in here that will fit you. Go on into the bathroom and find something for yourself."

I murmured a thank you and did as she asked. In the bag, I found a pair of jeans, a couple of pairs of shorts, a light green flowered sun dress, and a few T-shirts that looked like they would fit me much better than the yellow one did. I selected a pair of jeans and a dark green tank top, resisting the fear of showing my bare shoulders in public and giving in to the temptation of wearing something cool that didn't scratch at my skin. I put the rest of the clothes back in the bag, and went back out into the main room.

"Much better," Seton said appreciatively when I came out. "That green is gorgeous with your hair, by the way."

I blushed at the compliment. "Thank you," I murmured. "And thank you for letting me borrow these."

"Nope," she shook her head. "Not borrow.

Those are yours." When I protested, she laughed me off. "Remember, you're not to wear the Minions shirt except to bed when I give it back. And besides, those are all clothes I don't wear anymore. So don't worry, you're not putting me out."

I tried to argue with her, but she wouldn't have any of it. "The subject's closed," she said firmly. She reached into her back pocket and took out a cell phone, glancing at it briefly. "So, I'm guessing you haven't had dinner yet, right?"

In fact, I hadn't had lunch, either, but I didn't tell her that. The events of the day had my stomach in knots, anyway, so I didn't feel hungry, but I knew that if I didn't eat at some point, I'd be starving by bedtime. "No, I haven't."

"I've got a great idea," she said, her eyes twinkling. "I have had one crazy week, and I could really use a girls' night out. Let's you and me go out and get something to eat."

"I… um, I don't have any money," I admitted.

"Oh, I know," she said, smiling. "Don't worry about it. I've got cash. You can pay me back later if you really want to."

It was on the tip of my tongue to refuse, but Seton's smile was so open and accepting, I found myself relaxing a little. My conscience eased just a little at the hope that someday I'd be making my own money, and I'd be able to do pay her back for all of her kindness. As soon as I accepted, she grinned and slipped an arm through mine. "Great! Come on," she said. "I know just the place."

A half an hour later, we were seated in a booth at a bustling bar and grill called Hammie's. Seton introduced me to a friend of hers named Andi, a tall woman with almost platinum-blond hair working behind the bar, who immediately offered us a drink on the house. Seton ordered a margarita, and I frowned, not sure what to order for myself.

"Give her the same," Seton said to Andi, then glanced at me. "The margaritas here are fantastic." I didn't have the courage to tell her that I'd never tried alcohol before, so I stayed silent and thanked Andi for the drink.

When the waitress came, Seton ordered a burger and fries, and I ordered a club sandwich. Then she raised her glass in a toast. "To... hmm. To what? What should we toast to?" she asked.

"To the future," I said. I didn't know what it

held, but I hoped it would be better than the past.

We clinked glasses and drank. When the tart, strong liquid hit my throat, I started coughing so hard I almost dropped my glass. Seton pressed her lips together, clearly trying not to laugh.

"Um, Cherish, can I ask you something?"

"Of course," I wheezed at her, clapping myself on the chest and taking a long drink of water.

"Is that the first margarita you've ever had?"

There was no use trying to hide anything, I decided. "It's actually the first alcohol I've ever had," I admitted.

Her eyes went wide. "Really?" she asked. "I mean, I guess it's not that unusual, but… I don't know. I guess I just assumed…"

"No, it's okay." I had finally gotten my throat to start working again. "Where I come from, women aren't really allowed to drink."

"Where you come from?" she repeated. "You know, Levi didn't really tell me anything about you, other than that you showed up here because he knew your brother from when they were kids."

I opened my mouth to explain, but then shut it again. I wasn't sure how much to tell Seton about where I'd come from. On the one hand, my story was my own, but on the other, anything I told her about why I was here would tell her things about Levi, too. Things I wasn't sure he wanted anyone to know.

"I…" I began, then stopped. "Uh, I grew up in an FLDS community," I said reluctantly.

"FLDS?" she frowned. "Like, Latter-Day Saints? Mormons?"

"Fundamentalist Church of Jesus Christ of Latter-Day Saints," I corrected.

"Oh, okay, so Mormons don't drink alcohol," she nodded. "Right, I knew that."

Relieved, I said simply, "Not exactly like the Mormons, but yeah, the alcohol part is the same."

"So, are you still FLDS?" she asked, hesitating over the letters. "Because if so, I'm sorry I ordered you alcohol. I wouldn't have, if I'd known."

"I'm not sure what I am," I admitted. "But no, I don't think I'm FLDS anymore."

Our food came then, and for a few minutes, neither of us said much. I realized once I'd taken the first bite that I was ravenous, and had eaten most of my club sandwich and all of my fries before I knew it. Once I had eaten about half of my burger and demolished most of the fries, I sat back, sighed, and closed my eyes. "Thank you, Seton," I murmured. "That's the best meal I've had in a while."

I hadn't meant to say it; I was just so content that it slipped out. Seton looked at me for a long moment, and then simply said, "You're welcome. It's my pleasure. Like I said, I was in the mood for a girls' night out."

"Can I ask you a question?" I asked her.

"Sure, it's your turn," she said, smiling.

"Levi said you were someone's 'old lady'? The president's, I think? What does that mean?"

Seton laughed. "Yeah, the club president. His name is Greyson Stone. He and I are together."

"Like… married?" I ventured shyly.

She smiled. "Not yet, no. But soon, probably."

I nodded but didn't say anything. Part of me was shocked, but I knew that out in the world, lots of couples were together without being married. Besides, I reminded myself bitterly, if marriage out in the world meant what it had for me and so many other women at the Ranch, it was hardly all it was cracked up to be, anyway.

Seton told me a little more about Greyson and how they had met. Her eyes lit up as she described what he was like, and little aspects of his personality that she found endearing or funny. The way she talked, it was obvious she was completely in love with him. It made me a little wistful, and when the frowning image of Isaiah Whitehead came unbidden into my head, I pushed it back out firmly.

I took a few more tentative sips of the margarita. It was really strong, but it tasted sort of good once you knew what you were in for. As we finished our food, Seton changed the subject back to me. "So, you said that you came here to Lupine because your brother knew Levi growing up. Does that mean that Levi was in this FLDS community, too?"

My heart began to pound a little faster. Just as I suspected, Seton didn't know this about Levi. Which might mean that the others didn't either. "Um, yes,"

I admitted. "But he left a long time ago."

Her eyes widened. "Wow," she chuckled. "It's hard to imagine him being in a fundamentalist group."

I grinned shyly. "Yeah, he's changed a lot." I almost laughed at the mental image I had of how people at the Ranch would react if they saw him today, all tattoos, muscles, and leather.

Thankfully, Seton decided to drop the subject of Levi after that, and we spent the rest of the meal chatting about mundane things. I appreciated that she seemed to take care not to pry too much, or ask questions about where I'd be going tomorrow, when Levi had made it clear I had to leave. I had to fight a rising lump in my throat at the thought that I might not even see Seton again after tonight. In many ways, despite the fact that I'd only just met her, she felt like the first real friend I'd ever had. Almost all of the interactions I had had with the girls and women at the WFZ Ranch were completely superficial. Most of the conversations had to do with chores, or childbirth, or keeping a household, or the right way for a woman to be a devoted follower of God and a good wife to her husband. Just to talk with another woman about non-serious things like hair or clothes felt so foreign, but so relaxing, in a strange way. Far from feeling judged by her, or like she was watching me to make sure I wasn't straying from the path that God had chosen for me, I felt a level of freedom that I had never really felt before. It hurt my heart to think that a few days from now I'd probably never see her again, and she would quickly forget about me.

We stayed talking at Hammie's for almost three hours, and then Seton paid the bill and drove us back to the clubhouse. When we got inside, the bar was much louder than it had been. About twenty men, all tattooed, were laughing, drinking, and jostling each other. Most wore leather vests with patches that said, "Stone Kings MC." A handful of women, most of them scantily clad enough to make me blush, hung on the men. Rock music I didn't recognize played in the background.

Levi was there, standing with his back to me at a high top table with a few other men. "Grey!" Seton called, and a man standing next to him with close-cropped blond hair looked over at us. His face broke into a wide smile that softened his eyes as she ran to him. She flung her arms around his neck and he lifted her up, kissing her deeply as she kissed him back. I turned away, feeling strange at witnessing a moment that felt so intimate and private, and as I did, my eyes met Levi's. He stared at me for a few seconds, and as his eyes locked on mine I felt a strange sensation of warmth flood through me. The intense green of his eyes seemed to flash despite the dim light, almost as though they were boring inside me. My lips parted in surprise as my breath hitched in my throat. Then, as if nothing had happened, he glanced away, and I started breathing again, shivering slightly. I had never felt anything like it before, and all my nerve endings seemed to tingle, as though he had touched me instead of just looking at me.

"Cherish, come here and meet Grey!" Seton called. I walked up nervously, avoiding Levi's eyes.

"Hello," I said to the man holding Seton, raising my voice to be heard above the music. "Thank you for letting me stay overnight."

Grey nodded without smiling. "You're welcome. Levi said you were in a bit of a bind tonight."

My eyes flicked over to Levi, who was looking over at the bar now, seemingly ignoring the conversation.

"I promise I'll be gone tomorrow," I replied. Levi glanced at me briefly then, before turning away again.

Seton waved a hand dismissively. "You don't have to go tomorrow, Cherish." She looked up at Grey, whose arm had curved around her possessively. "I like having her around. It's nice to have another girl to talk to."

Grey didn't say anything, so I didn't reply. Seton smiled over at me reassuringly, and I silently thanked her with my eyes. Levi was still pretending to ignore the conversation, but of course, he didn't need to speak. He had already made it very clear he didn't want me here. Even though I still had no idea what I was going to do, I wouldn't stay any longer than tomorrow without his consent. After all, it was only because of Levi's kindness that I was here in the first place, and I didn't want to be any more trouble to him than I already had been. It wasn't just that he didn't want the trouble of some strange woman hanging around. Without him telling me, I somehow sensed that my presence was a door to his past that he wanted to remain firmly closed.

Tomorrow, I decided, I would be on my way. I didn't know how, or where, but I'd figure it out after a good night's sleep.

CHAPTER 6

Levi

Grey gave me a goddamn earful about letting Cherish stay at the clubhouse overnight. Especially because I basically refused to give him any details about who she was, where she was from, or how I knew her.

Luckily, I had called Seton to get Cherish set up with a change of clothes and to help her get settled in for the night. I had only done it because I couldn't figure out what the hell to do with her myself, but it ended up being an even better decision than I'd realized at the time. Seton took Cherish out for some food, and by the time they got back to the clubhouse, they were as thick as thieves. And once Seton was on board, I knew it was okay about Cherish, at least for the night. Greyson Stone could make a grown man piss his pants with just a look, but damn if Seton didn't have him wrapped around her little finger.

When the two women came back from their dinner, a bunch of the club officers were hanging around a high-top table near the bar, talking details about a meet with the head of the Aztecs cartel that was to happen the next day. I hadn't noticed the two women come in until I heard Seton's voice calling out Grey's name. I looked up to see her running toward him like they hadn't seen each other in weeks. She wrapped herself around him, and Grey lifted her off the ground with a smile he reserved only for her, kissing her in front of all of us like there was no one else around. On the one hand, it was kind of awkward. I mean, life at the clubhouse was hardly chaste, and I had seen more than one man flip a woman over on the pool table and have at her like there weren't two dozen other people in the same room. But that was just sex. This was something else entirely, and the intimacy between them felt private in a completely different way. But even as I squirmed a little to see them like that, shit, I was happy for Grey. I couldn't deny that Seton made him happy, and even though I had had my doubts about her at first, she was actually a pretty great person. They were clearly crazy about each other, and Seton made Grey less of a brooding fuck to be around, which was all good by me.

As I looked away from the Seton and Grey show, I happened to glance at Cherish as she walked shyly toward our table. My eyes widened in surprise. She had on a different pair of jeans now that hugged her ass, and she was wearing a tight little green tank top that showed off a body I could never have imagined under the formless yellow T-shirt she was wearing when I met her. Alarm bells sounded loud inside my head as I sprouted wood like a goddamn teenage boy at the sight of her.

Holy hell. She was freaking gorgeous. I doubted she had any idea of the effect that she would have on a man in those clothes. If she did, I doubt she could have just put them on and stepped out into the open. There was something about the green of her shirt and the way her dark hair framed her face that brought out the creaminess of her skin, and made me want to taste her, devour her, pull down her jeans and her panties and fuck her with my tongue until she came screaming my name.

Shit. I needed to get some goddamn control of myself. I shifted uncomfortably from one leg to the other and moved a little closer to the table, thankful that its shadow would hide my throbbing erection. I took a long swig of beer from the bottle in front of me and reminded myself that she'd be gone in the morning. All I had to deal with was one night, and then I'd hopefully never see her again.

As much as I tried to make myself ignore her, I couldn't help but notice that Cherish seemed a little self-conscious as she walked toward us. I couldn't blame her. Even though her clothes happened to fit her like a goddamn glove, they were hardly what you'd call revealing. But for her, she must have felt like she was practically naked. The community we'd grown up in didn't allow women to expose skin below the neck, and regarded female nudity as of the Devil. Modesty was taught to women as the most important virtue. She had to be making a supreme effort to get used to wearing clothes that weren't specifically designed to cover up everything that made her look like a woman. If she knew that the mere sight of her made me want to take her upstairs and fuck her, she'd probably freak out and go try to find a garbage bag to put on or something.

It had been a long damn time since I'd thought about the community I'd grown up in, but now I found myself remembering how constricting life there was for the women, even more so than for the men. Cherish said she had been married, but I knew that didn't mean much in terms of her sexual experience, or comfort with her own body. Hell, I doubted very strongly that she had ever been actually naked in front of anyone before in her life since the day she was born. Both women and men were required to wear temple garments at all times, which were underwear that covered them from above the elbows to just above the knees. Sex with her husband was most likely done in the dark, a simple affair of him pushing up her nightgown and doing whatever the fuck he wanted while she just sat and took it.

My blood started to boil in my veins as I imagined Isaiah Whitehead pounding out his lust on Cherish, with no interest in her pleasure or even her consent. I knew without knowing what their life had probably been like. Hell, I'd seen it myself growing up with my own father and his three wives. The youngest one was thirteen when I left. She was a "spiritual marriage," which meant that he was supposed to wait until she was old enough to be considered an adult to have his way with her, but of course nobody actually did that. I remembered hearing the muffled cries coming from her bedroom the first night he brought her home. The next day, her pale, frightened face as she helped my mother make the breakfast was the first nail in the coffin of my decision to leave the WFZ Ranch.

The expression on my face must have revealed my angry thoughts, because Cherish stopped short when her eyes met mine. "Oh," she said, taking a step back. I realized she must have thought I was angry at her, and couldn't decide whether it was better to let her keep thinking that.

"You got a change of clothes," I said in a neutral voice.

She gave me an uncertain half-smile. "Yes, Seton has been really nice. She brought me a few different things. She says I'm not allowed to give them back."

That made me smile in spite of myself. "Well, Seton's no one to be trifled with. If that's what she says, that's the way it's gonna be."

She looked down at the table and said in a quiet voice, "Thank you for letting me stay the night. I know I'm not really welcome."

Goddamnit. My belly knotted with a regret I didn't want to feel. I didn't want to hurt Cherish. I just didn't want her here. It was nothing personal. But there was no doubt that she needed to be gone, tomorrow. An outlaw motorcycle club was no place for someone like her. Especially given the club's current situation.

"It's not that," I said gruffly. "It's just better if you don't hang around."

She nodded and made a brave attempt at a smile. "I understand. I promise not to be in anyone's way."

"Oh, please, you're not in anyone's way," Seton cut in. I turned to see her lean into Grey's enveloping arm. "The men can be a little gruff at times, but don't let them scare you," she winked at Cherish. "They're all just a bunch of pussycats."

"Seton," Grey began in a warning tone.

She rolled her eyes playfully. "Yes, I know you're as tough as they come, Greyson Stone. But honestly, you'd never harm a hair on a woman's head. So don't give me that menacing voice. I know better."

"Jesus," Grey sighed, kissing her forehead. "What I have to put up with."

"You know you love it," Seton teased back. She unwrapped herself from Grey's embrace and turned to Cherish. "Come on, honey, let's go upstairs and give these men a chance to finish their shop talk."

We watched the two of them head up the staircase together, and I tried not to stare at Cherish's ass.

Grey eyed me speculatively. "You sure you're not gonna tell me who she is?"

I was silent for a moment. "Just someone from my past."

Grey didn't seem satisfied with my answer, but he let it drop, and called out to the other officers to join us at the table. He wanted to give them the final details of our meet up with Lalo, the leader of the Aztecs cartel, which was to happen the following day.

A situation had developed, and it was time to get to the bottom of it. After quite a few years of relative calm and quiet, the Stone Kings had recently suffered two unexplained violent attacks that had happened in our territory. The first one had cost the life of our brother Hammer, who was Grey's best friend since childhood. The second, a drive-by shooting at a diner a couple of towns over, had injured a couple of our men, and also some of the townspeople. The trouble was, in both instances, we didn't know who had been behind the attacks.

The drive-by at the diner, a club hangout called Maisie's, had escalated the situation considerably. True, none of the brothers had been seriously injured in the attack, but a couple of the people in the community had also been hurt, one of whom was still in the hospital. Our club was careful to maintain good relationships with the civilians that lived on our turf, and for the most part, we coexisted peacefully, thanks in part to some of the kids' charity runs and other events we organized in and around Lupine. For the most part, they left us alone and we left them alone.

An attack on us that wounded the citizens of the area risked eroding the goodwill that we'd worked hard to maintain over the years. Even though the attack had been meant for us, the public didn't know enough to distinguish between different motorcycle clubs easily. When violence happened involving the club and it touched them, all they knew was that our presence in the community was the reason.

The Stone Kings hadn't had any serious turf wars

in quite a while. A few years ago, Grey had brokered a truce with the Aztecs cartel that allowed them passage through our territory to transport their product — at first drugs, but since pot legalization, mostly weapons now. Our club had a good working relationship with the Aztecs and their leader Lalo, and if I didn't quite trust him, I trusted that keeping the terms of the truce was in everyone's mutual best interest.

Recently, another outlaw club, called the Cannibals, had joined Lalo's cartel. Their leader, Skull, seemed like a shifty-ass motherfucker to me, and Grey and the other officers tended to share my opinion. The meet with Lalo tomorrow was about Skull and the Cannibals, and Grey's objective was to get some sort of read on Lalo's relationship to them. It seemed to us that Skull and the Cannibals were the most logical culprits behind the attacks on our club, and if it turned out that it was them, justice would have to be dealt. But if we hit the Cannibals, we essentially were hitting the cartel, as well, potentially destroying a relationship that had worked well for everyone, and starting a war that could blow up in everyone's faces.

"I think we need to take everyone we can to this meet," Trigger, the VP, argued as he lit up a smoke.

"It could turn ugly, and I don't want our men caught out there unprotected." I knew he was thinking about what had happened with Hammer, caught out in the open unawares, with only our brother Jethro to cover him. Jethro had turned out to be a cowardly piece of shit, and left Hammer to be shot and die alone. Even though Jethro had been dealt with, and would never betray anyone again, it still left a lingering taste of anger in all our mouths.

I lifted my chin toward Trig in agreement. "Not a bad idea." I knew that in a way, bringing most of our men to a meet that was supposed to just be an informal chat between presidents ran a pretty good risk of escalating tensions, but hell, I didn't give a shit. We still didn't know who was behind the attacks on us, and until we did, I wasn't comfortable with a group of our officers going anywhere without a lot of backup.

Grey seemed inclined to disagree, but then thought better of it. "Okay," he nodded. "But we're gonna leave a few of the men here at the clubhouse while we're gone. I'm not gonna leave this place unprotected."

"You think Lalo knows who's behind the attacks?" Winger asked.

Grey shook his head. "I don't think he's behind it, if that's what you're asking. If he does know something, he's taking a pretty big risk by protecting them. A war with us would cut off his main transport route indefinitely, and he knows it. Seems like a pretty fucking stupid move, unless the people he's protecting are even more important to him than we are."

"Goddamnit, this pisses me off," Trigger roared suddenly, slamming his fist down on the table. "I want to know who's behind this!"

"We all do, brother," Grey replied. His face was a careful mask of calm, but behind it, I could see his jaw tensing in anger. "We all do. And when we figure it out, there'll be payback."

I shared Trigger's fury, and I knew that behind it was the frustration that grew out of feeling helpless. The Stone King were men of action. The weeks of not being able to make those responsible pay for their crimes was beginning to take their toll on the club.

As our club president, one of Grey's strengths was his ability to think tactically, to keep his emotions from clouding his judgment. He had confided to me that he believed whoever was responsible for the anonymous attacks was trying to destabilize the club — to sow discord among the brothers and make us weaker, by keeping us guessing as to who was targeting us and why. If that was the case, Grey's timetable before it started working was limited. The only thing that kept some of the more warlike brothers like Trigger in check was the knowledge that our president had lost his best friend in the attacks. They may have been impatient at Grey's slow, deliberate approach, but I don't think any of us were in doubt that eventually, someone would pay for Hammer's death.

I hoped their faith in him would hold for long enough for us to figure out who it was.

CHAPTER 7

Cherish

Seton followed me up to the apartment, chattering away gaily, and I did my best to pay attention. But frankly, all the excitement and stress of the past twenty-four hours had gotten to me, and I was struggling to stay awake. It was barely nine o'clock, but all I could think about was climbing in between the sheets and closing my eyes.

"Now, when you get up tomorrow morning, feel free to go downstairs into the clubhouse kitchen area," Seton was saying. "There should be enough groceries in the fridge to make yourself a decent enough breakfast. And there's always coffee." Her eyes twinkled. "Don't be surprised if you get roped into making breakfast for one of the men if they wander in and see you cooking. You can cook, right?"

I simply nodded my head. I'd been cooking for entire families for about as long as I could remember, but I was too tired to tell her that and face any questions about why.

Seton helped me turn down the bed, and made sure I had everything I needed. "Do you have a toothbrush? Toothpaste?"

I assured her I did, and then remembered something. "I forgot to pack a nightgown," I said.

"Oh, well," she shrugged. "You can just wear that shirt, and your underwear, I suppose, if you need to wear something. It's warm enough you wouldn't need anything at all, if you didn't want."

I had never considered the idea that some people might sleep in the nude. I glanced at the bed, where who knew how many others had slept before me. I'd keep my shirt and underwear on.

Seton stood and stretched her arms above her head. "I'll come back tomorrow to see how you're doing," she smiled at me. "Maybe early afternoon? It's my day off from work. I can take you for a tour around Lupine." She had told me she worked as an apprentice chef at one of the restaurants in town.

It was on the tip of my tongue to say yes, but then I remembered something. "I might not be here," I said slowly. "I'm only supposed to stay until tomorrow. They might make me leave first thing in the morning."

Seton laughed and waved her hand dismissively. "Don't worry about that," she said. "They're not going to kick you out. I promise."

I tried to believe her, but it didn't seem likely that Levi would let me stay, and in any case, I had promised him I would leave tomorrow. Even though I didn't have the slightest idea what I would do, I didn't want to break my word to him. Even though I would probably never see him again after tomorrow, I didn't want him to think badly of me. Despite his wild look and his tattoo-covered skin, I respected him. I was just starting to realize how hard it was going to be to leave the WFZ community and start fresh without anyone to help me. He had made a clean break, and had a new life, a new identity, and he had been even younger than I was now when he did it. I hoped I could be half as brave as he had been.

Seton said goodbye to me, and I locked the door securely behind her. The apartment was quiet except for the murmur of voices and the muted boom of music below me. The noise was comforting; even though I was alone, I knew there were people not far away, and that they were having fun. Although I was in the presence of near-strangers, I felt safer here than I had in days. I stripped off my jeans, pulled my bra off from under my shirt, and climbed into bed, groaning in pleasure again at the softness of the bed. I turned off the light and stared at the shadows the light coming in through the window made on the walls. Before I knew it, I was asleep.

My dreams were fitful and full of strange mixtures of my past and my present. In one of them, Levi was at the WFZ Ranch, dressed in the conservative clothing typical of the men in that community. His tattoos were visible above the collar of his shirt and below his cuffs, and I kept wondering why no one was saying anything about them. He came to our house to see to my husband Isaiah, and I busied myself by working in the kitchen as they sat at the table together talking. From the moment he sat down, Levi's eyes never left me. Even with my back to him, I could feel his gaze heating me from the inside, until I felt like I was made of molten lava. My body shook with the fear that Isaiah would notice him looking at me, but at the same time my skin tingled until it felt as sensitive as if Levi were actually touching me.

I woke in a sweat the next morning, an ache between my legs unlike anything I'd ever felt before. I sat up, my breathing shallow, and tried to shake the sensation of guilt that had followed me from my dream. The throb of what I dimly realized must be desire followed me into the bathroom. I ran cold water to splash my face and brushed my hair out of the tangled nest it had become with all of my tossing and turning. There was a clock on the wall above the bed, so I knew it was a little before ten-thirty in the morning. My stomach growled suddenly, and I remembered that my last meal had been over fourteen hours ago.

The thumping music that had been my

background noise last night as I fell asleep had been replaced this morning by the low murmur of men talking downstairs. I went to the paper bag Seton had brought me the night before, dressed in the same pair of jeans and a light pink T-shirt that I found, and steeled myself to go downstairs and face a group of strange men who didn't know me from Eve.

The kitchen wasn't hard to find, as it was down a short hall behind the bar area. I scurried through the main room of the bar, careful not to meet the eyes of any of the men there, and breathed a sigh of relief that the kitchen was deserted at this hour. I found some pre-ground coffee and some filters in a cupboard above an automatic drip coffee maker. I loved the smell of coffee, but members of our community weren't allowed to drink caffeine. I hesitated, almost closing the cupboard door, and then reminded myself that I didn't belong to the WFZ Ranch anymore. It was almost dizzying, all of the small new freedoms this new life had. Half-giddy, I put some water in the drip maker for about half a pot, and tried to estimate how much ground coffee I needed to put in the maker. Luckily, the package had directions so I didn't mess it up too badly.

Next, I looked in the refrigerator, and was surprised to see eggs, milk, and even a couple of packets of sausage. My stomach rumbled again, growing more impatient. I found a bowl, and cracked two eggs into it for scrambling. I located two skillets, a small and a medium, in another cabinet next to the stove, put the eggs into one, and a couple of the sausages in the other. I turned on the stove and stood there waiting for things to cook, something about the repetitive nature of these domestic tasks, which I had done so many times before, helping to dissipate the lingering unsettledness I had been feeling since waking up.

A couple of minutes later, one of the men from the bar wandered into the room. He looked to be about my age, with brown, wavy hair that curled around his ears and a square, handsome jaw. Like the other men I had seen, he had tattoos, but fewer than most, and certainly fewer than Levi. He was wearing a clean white T-shirt and loose jeans over motorcycle boots.

"Mmm, smells good," he said, grinning. "You sharing?"

Even though he was much taller than I was and I knew he was a club member, there was something about him that made him feel a little less intimidating than the other men I had seen. Maybe it was because of his apparent proximity to my age. I smiled back at him shyly and said, "I can. Scrambled eggs and sausage, if you want."

"I want," he nodded. Pulling out a chair from the square fake wood and metal kitchen table, he flipped it around and sat so that his arms were resting on the back. I walked back to the refrigerator and pulled the eggs back out along with the sausage. "These are just about done," I told him, and smiled. "My name's Cherish."

"Cal," he replied, raising his chin in a sort of half-nod. "Nice to meet you."

"You, too."

"You don't seem like the typical girl we see around here," he continued in an amused voice. "How'd you end up at an MC clubhouse?"

I reddened. "Uh… I'm just here until later today. I… just needed a place to stay."

"Who brought you here?" he asked. I could tell he was not going to be the type to let this go easily, but I tried to give him as little as I could.

"Um... no one brought me here. But my brother knew Levi when we were kids, so I took a chance that he might help me out."

"Levi?" he said, one eyebrow shooting up quizzically. "You know Levi? Man, I can't even really imagine him as a kid. What was he like?"

"I don't know," I said honestly. "He left... uh, left town when I was really young, so I don't really remember him."

"Huh," Cal murmured. He nodded slowly, considering. By then, the first batch of eggs and sausage was ready, and I grabbed a plate and set them before him. The food seemed to distract him from any more conversation about Levi. I watched him eat for a moment, smiling as he made appreciative noises and gave me a thumbs up. Then I put some more eggs and sausage on for myself.

The coffee maker beeped, startling me, and I realized it must be ready. I took a mug down from the cupboard, poured myself half a cup, and took an experimental sip. It was hot, so hot it almost burned my lips, and bitter. I wasn't sure what I thought of it yet. It certainly tasted different than it smelled. I raised the cup to take second taste when another man came in. I recognized him from the night before, when Seton and I had gotten back from dinner. He was tall and dark, with coal black hair and piercing brown eyes. His voice was a deep bass, and as soon as he spoke I remembered hearing him talking to Greyson and Levi the night before.

"Cal, you gonna give me a hand out back?" he asked from the doorway.

Cal nodded and swallowed a forkful of egg. "Just about done here, Trig. Cherish here was nice enough to make me a delicious and healthy second breakfast."

The man Cal had called Trig looked at me speculatively. "Cal's already got you earning your keep, eh?"

I blushed. "I was just making some breakfast for myself and he came in, so I thought I'd make some for him, as well. Seton told me I could help myself. I hope that's not a problem."

Trig chuckled, a surprisingly merry sound coming from such a dangerous looking man. "Hey, when the prez's old lady tells you can do something, you can do it."

"You met See, eh?" Cal asked. He stood up and

brought his plate to the sink. "She's my sister."

Now there was a surprise. "Really? She's been really nice to me. She brought me these clothes when I showed up last night, and even took me out for dinner."

"Oh, yeah, actually I recognize that shirt," Cal grinned. "Ha, it looks better on you."

I laughed. "I doubt that, but thank you anyway."

Trig looked at Cal and gave him a half-joking look of warning. "Watch it, brother. Don't forget Levi told us that she was strictly off limits. Keep your pants on."

I realized belatedly that Cal might have been trying to flirt with me. I didn't know whether to be flattered or embarrassed. Thankfully, my eggs and sausage were finally done, and I busied myself by getting another plate from the cupboard and serving myself.

Trig clapped Cal on the back and said, "Well, miss..."

"Cherish," I told him.

"Well, miss Cherish, we'll be on our way and let

you eat before Cal tries to put the moves on you." Cal thanked me for the food and then they were gone, leaving me alone to finally fill my rumbling stomach.

As I ate, I thought about what Trig had said. *Don't forget Levi told us that she was strictly off limits.* The two men, Cal and Trig, had both been unwaveringly polite to me. I wondered how much Levi had to do with that, and how they would have acted if he hadn't given them a warning. I silently thanked him for protecting me from whatever he thought I needed protecting from.

Almost as if he had read my mind and knew I was thinking about him, Levi walked into the kitchen just as I was finishing up my plate of eggs. "Trigger said you were in here," he murmured by way of greeting. Instead of sitting down, he leaned against the wall nearest the doorway. "Sleep well?"

"Yes, thank you," I replied. I blushed as the dream involving him flashed briefly into my mind. My heart began to flutter in my chest.

"Good," he said, and then was silent.

I stood and picked up my plate to take it to the sink. "I want to thank you again for letting me stay here last night, Levi," I said softly. I looked into his eyes, and tried to ignore the growing surge of heat at my core. "I know you didn't have to. And I know it probably caused you some trouble."

His gaze traveled briefly over me before coming back to my face. "Don't mention it," he murmured gruffly.

Feeling awkward, I turned away from him and busied myself by turning on the water to wash the dishes. "I want you to know I'll be out of here as soon as I figure out what I'm going to do next. I promise I'll be gone by nightfall." I had no idea how my situation could possibly change by nightfall, and the thought of leaving without money or a plan absolutely terrified me. But I had given Levi my word, and I wasn't going to go back on it.

He shifted from one leg to another, looking suddenly uncomfortable. "Look, you don't have to leave right away. I know you really haven't had time to figure much out."

"No, it's okay," I said, shaking my head. "I know it's a burden to have me here. I shouldn't have imposed on you in the first place."

He sighed. "It's not a burden, Cherish. You

barely take up any space at all."

"It is," I repeated stubbornly. "I know I don't really... *fit* here." I laughed. "Obviously. And the few people I've met have been so nice to me." *Thanks to you.* "But still, they've had to go out of their way for me, and I can't really do anything to pay them back for it." I looked down into the sink absently. "I'm not used to taking favors from people."

A silence passed between us. Levi detached himself from the wall and slumped into the chair Cal had vacated. "Cherish," he began, and then paused before continuing. "I'm glad you contacted me. If it got you out of there. I'm glad."

I turned from the sink, grabbing a towel to dry my hands. I looked at the floor, not quite daring to meet his eyes. I stood there for a moment, reflecting. Finally, I glanced at him and sighed softly. "I think, to be honest, I just needed the idea of having some place to go, to help me decide to finally leave. You know? Just so I had a destination in mind when I left the Ranch."

His brow furrowed, considering. "Yeah." After a moment, he added. "It's not easy to take the first step."

"No. It's not." It felt strange, to be having this conversation with someone who was at once a total stranger and the one person in the world who would understand what I was saying. "I think the idea of just leaving, with no way to say, 'I'm going *to* this place'… It would have felt like jumping off a cliff." My voice diminished to almost a whisper. "I'm not sure I would have had the courage to do it, otherwise."

Levi was looking at me intensely now, his expression unreadable. "Why did you leave?" he asked suddenly. "I mean, what was the final thing that pushed you?"

"I'm not sure," I lied. But something inside me was telling me to give him the truth. It felt wrong to lie to him, after he had helped me. And in a way, maybe it would be good to say it to someone. I paused a moment to gather my courage, then shook my head. "No, that's not true. I do know what it was." My eyes met his, and I forced myself not to look away.

"I was married to a man who has four children," I began. "I was his second wife. His first one, my sister wife — her name is Carolyn — she believes in everything they teach you about what women should do. That they should only be concerned with their roles as godly, obedient spouses. Except she hates me." I shrugged. "I'm not sure why. Maybe it's because her children get along with me so well. I'm sort of more like an older sister to them. And maybe, too, because once I was married to Isaiah, he shared my bed more often than he shared hers."

My face flamed red. I had never spoken about sex to anyone, let alone a man I barely knew. I took a deep breath and plunged ahead with my story.

"I was actually married once before, before Isaiah. When I was sixteen. Abram died after we'd been married a little over two years," I continued. "Luckily, he was so old when we married that he wasn't really able to... well, you know." I looked at the floor. "So, I was a virgin when I got married to Isaiah at nineteen. I didn't really know how good I'd had it with Abram until my wedding night with Isaiah. Since I had been married once before, no one really thought to explain to me what was going to happen." I drew my arms protectively around myself at the memory of that night. "As I said, Isaiah shared my bed most nights after that first one. He... he beat me if ever I didn't want to sleep with him, so I learned not to object."

I risked a glance at Levi before I went on. His face was dark, his jaw clenched. I looked back down at the floor and continued.

"The thing is, Isaiah's oldest daughter by Carolyn is fourteen now. Her name is Abigail. She's a sweet girl, pretty and obedient. And..." My voice began to crack, and I swallowed painfully. "And Isaiah just made the decision that she's to be married off to a man of forty-two. Carolyn agrees with him, and poor Abigail..." My lip trembled. "Poor Abigail doesn't know what she's in for." A tear rolled down my cheek, then another. "I realized that when I had children, they would be Isaiah's, too. And he would make the same decisions for them. For any daughters I had." A sob escaped me, and I shook my head as I fought for words. "I just couldn't stay, knowing that was my future, my children's future. I just couldn't."

Levi looked stricken. "Jesus. Cherish... I don't know what to say."

"No. No, it's fine," I sniffled, grabbing a paper towel from the rack and wiping at my eyes. "It's... it's actually sort of a relief to talk about it. I've been thinking about it for so long, without any way to say it out loud." I sighed shakily. "It's a little like an escape valve." I smiled at him weakly through my tears. "Thanks."

For a moment, neither of us spoke. What else was there to say?

"Well," I finally said, to break the silence. "I should finish cleaning these skillets. Then I should go wash up. I think Seton is planning to come see me in a little while."

Levi stood. "I'll let you get to it, then." For a moment, he seemed to be on the verge of saying something else, but then he turned and was gone. I sighed and turned back to the dishes, emotionally drained by the unexpectedly serious conversation with Levi. I had never had such a deeply personal conversation with anyone before, let alone a man who wasn't even related to me. I wasn't quite sure what had gotten into me. I hoped he hadn't regretted asking me about my decision to leave.

After finishing up in the kitchen, I went upstairs and took another long shower, which made me feel somewhat better. Once I had brushed out my hair and gotten dressed, I found a stray paperback in the apartment and tried to distract myself with it. I knew I should probably be thinking about what my next steps were, but frankly the idea was so overwhelming

I didn't know where to start. I was hoping that maybe a conversation with Seton would give me some ideas. Maybe there was someplace in town that took in women who didn't have any place to stay.

A little after one o'clock, I heard footsteps on the stairs and a knock on my door. I opened it to find Seton in a bright white camisole and jean shorts, looking radiant. "Hey, Cherish! Ready to come shopping with me?"

I wasn't sure what we would be shopping for, but I didn't care. Just tagging along with her sounded fine by me. I'd pick her brain for ideas while we were out, and hopefully by the time we got back to the clubhouse, I'd have a plan.

CHAPTER 8

Levi

A couple of hours after my conversation with Cherish, and I was still practically shaking with fury. I left the clubhouse almost immediately after she went upstairs, and got on my bike without saying a word to anyone about where I was going. I needed to clear my head and calm myself down before I tore the first unfortunate son of a bitch I happened to come across a new asshole.

I drove fast and recklessly, almost daring the road to fuck with me. I flew out of town at a full thirty miles over the speed limit, and didn't stop until I finally came to a lush valley of evergreens with meandering, winding roads — a rarity in this part of the state. I slowed and took the curves at a steep lean, letting the tension ebb away as I concentrated on being one with the bike. On the far side of the valley, I stopped in a pool of cool shade by the side of the road and parked the bike. I still wasn't calmed down, so I lit a cigarette from the pack inside my shirt and paced a little as I smoked it.

The story that Cherish told me had opened up some very old wounds that I'd thought had finally healed. Her version of why she finally decided to leave the Ranch was so similar in some ways to my own that it almost defied belief. It was a story I'd never told anybody, and I had tried so hard to forget it over the years that it felt as though I had just reopened a deep cut and exposed the raw nerves underneath.

I saw how hard it had been for Cherish to hold back her tears as she told me her story. She had been scarred by her life at the Ranch in many of the same ways I had been. I had been a fool not to realize that from the beginning. Just the mere fact that she had had the guts to pack up and leave everything she knew should have told me that, without her having to open up her heart and spill it out right in front of me.

When I got tired of pacing, I straddled the bike, leaned back, and lit another smoke. Gone were any traces of my initial anger at Cherish showing up unannounced at the clubhouse. I still knew she would eventually have to leave, but I was glad that she had chosen to take a chance by coming to Lupine. I figured that she was probably right when she said she might not have had the courage to get out otherwise.

I was happy she had somehow heard my name, that knowing someone else had made it out had somehow given her some hope. The only trouble was, there was something about her that kept me thinking inappropriate thoughts about all sorts of things I wanted to do to her. I didn't know what it was; she had a basic innocence about her that told me she'd probably never had a man give her pleasure before. But at the same time, somehow she had this effortless sexiness about her that drove me wild just to be around her. The way her hips naturally swayed when she walked, just begging your eyes to watch… My hands frankly itched to reach out and cup her ass, pulling her against my hard cock. I fairly itched to hear her start whimpering and pressing her wet, hot need against me…

Fuck. Just like that, I was hard as a rock. It felt like I had been pretty much constantly since she emerged for the first time yesterday in the clothes she'd gotten from Seton. Hell, if she could make just jeans and a simple tank top look that good, imagine what she'd look like with a tight little dress that showed off all her curves and left nothing to the imagination. The video running in my head switched to her in a little black mini-dress with sky-high heels, lying on my bed as I slid the skirt up around her thighs. I could hear her breath, shallow and rapid, as she parted her legs slightly and I found the hot, wet center of her and began to stroke her clit…

Goddamn. Okay. I needed to stop thinking about her. I was isolated enough here to get away with jacking off and being done with it, but I needed to stop entertaining thoughts of fucking Cherish. At least until she was gone and safely out of my life.

I sat looking at the pines and brush in silence and thinking about how fucked up life could be. I stayed out there for a couple of hours, fighting off dueling impulses to either drive to the WFZ Ranch and bomb the place to kingdom come, or just chuck everything and go build myself a cabin somewhere up in the mountains so I wouldn't have to deal with people and their complicated, fucked up lives anymore.

Eventually, when I knew I couldn't put it off any longer, I sat up, pointed my bike in the opposite direction, and headed back to the clubhouse. We had the meet with the leader of the Aztec cartel this afternoon, and as much as club business was the last thing on my mind right now, I couldn't let down my brothers. I needed to be there to see how Lalo reacted to Grey telling him the Cannibals were probably responsible for the attacks on our club.

The meet didn't go well. Lalo Hernandez, the leader of the Aztecs cartel, was a short, stocky man about fifty years old, with black hair that was just starting to show gray at the temples. He had a thin mustache and a penchant for expensive suits. The Stone Kings had had a decent working relationship with Lalo and the cartel for a number of years. The truce that was set up by Grey's dad when he was president was solid, and had held for as long as I had been a Stone King with no major problems.

The first sign that there might be some tension was that Lalo showed up not just with his men, but with Skull, the president of the Cannibals, in tow.

Skull stood in a group of other men who seemed to be all Aztecs. When he saw us arrive his mouth widened in an arrogant smile. He lifted his chin toward Grey in a mocking salute.

Since Grey had told Lalo that he wanted to talk about the Cannibals, the move to bring Skull was, if not a line in the sand, at least pretty fucking concerning. Luckily, Grey didn't have much trouble convincing Lalo to leave everyone but himself and three of his officers outside the abandoned depot where we were meeting. Grey, Trig, Moose, and I followed them inside, leaving the other men to stand guard and keep watch on the Aztecs and Skull.

"What is it you want to talk to me about, Grey?" Lalo asked stiffly. He was wearing a dark pinstriped suit that looked like it cost more than my bike, his hands clasped in front of him.

Grey frowned and explained the situation. "We may have a problem with the new members of your cartel, Lalo. I came to you because your organization and mine have always had a good professional relationship. Our truce is strong and has been for a long time. I'm sure neither one of us wants to do anything to jeopardize it."

Lalo nodded, and his expression became less

stony. "Yes, that is true. The trust has been important for both of us for a long time."

"How well do you know the new president of the Cannibals?" Grey asked pointedly.

"Skull? He came to me some months ago, not long after he was named president of the Cannibals," Lalo replied. "He had a deal that he wanted to renegotiate between us regarding moving arms shipments. He made an offer that was very advantageous to us, and so I accepted."

"And you didn't know him before that?"

"No," Lalo answered.

Grey nodded. "We have reason to believe that the Cannibals are behind two recent attacks on our club. One of them killed a brother. The other one was out in the open, and injured some civilians."

"What makes you think it is the Cannibals?" Lalo asked smoothly.

"There's no other club who would have any reason to do anything like this." Grey shook his head. "The first attack happened not long after Skull took over as president of the Cannibals, and I

believe not long after their club joined your cartel."
He cocked his head at Lalo. "If it was the Cannibals,
their actions would be breaking our truce."

"Why would the Cannibals do such a thing?
What would they have to gain from it?" His voice
was dismissive.

"You tell me." Grey crossed his arms. "I know
Skull even less well than you. Maybe he's just crazy,
and has no motive at all. But more than likely, he
does have one. And if you don't know what it is,
then I suggest you better figure it out. Because if he
goes down, he'll take your cartel down with him."

Lalo made a noise of impatience. "This is a
serious accusation, Grey."

"I am not accusing anyone. Yet," Grey corrected
him. "But the men who attacked us were too
cowardly to leave a signature. When we find out who
they were, we will have to take action. Justice will
have to be served. If it is the Cannibals, the question
in our minds is gonna be whether the Aztecs knew
about it. You know what this could mean."

"Are you threatening me, Greyson?" Lalo asked,
his expression turning dark, dangerous.

"I am not threatening you, Lalo." Grey's words were frank. "I am telling you as a business associate that your alliance with Skull may threaten something much larger."

Lalo's voice was tight. "What are you suggesting?"

"I suggest that you find out what the Cannibals' relationship is to those attacks before I do. And I suggest that when you find that relationship out, you tell me and give our club a chance to mete out justice before this thing blows up in all of our faces and starts a war."

Lalo's face turned to stone. "I believe we are finished here," he said. He nodded once to the man on his right, and the four of them filed out silently as we watched them leave.

"Well, that went well," Trigger said sarcastically when they were gone.

"What do we do now?" I asked.

"We wait," Grey said.

Trigger swore. "How long?"

"As long as we have to," Grey retorted, his voice

flinty. Trigger didn't push it.

The sounds of cars and motorcycles leaving reached our ears, and we lingered, waiting for them to be gone before we turned toward the exit to rejoin our brothers. It wasn't surprising, in a way, that Lalo hadn't been all that receptive to the accusations against the Cannibals. After all, we had no proof. His inclusion of Skull among the men waiting outside didn't prove anything one way or another, either. I resisted the urge to punch something in frustration. I wondered how long the Stone Kings would be willing to hold off from acting before tensions started to rise.

When we got back to the club, the sun was just beginning to set. I had been so caught up in club business that I'd forgotten Cherish had planned to be gone by now, and my stomach clenched at the thought that I might have missed her. But just as we had parked the bikes and gone inside, Seton emerged from the kitchen and walked toward the four of us.

"Greyson," she began, and nodded her head at the rest of us in greeting. "I asked Cherish to stay for the rest of the week."

He swore softly and looked at her with a frown. "Seton, this isn't a halfway house."

But Seton was fierce. "She has no place to go, Greyson," she said in a voice that brooked no argument. "Believe me, the last thing she wants to do is inconvenience us all. But she's got no one. You've got to give her a little time to get on her feet." Her eyes widened. "She told me that she comes from a fundamentalist Latter-Day Saints community in Arizona. Like, sister wives and stuff." Seton's gaze flickered toward me for a moment, and I looked away. "Can you imagine how hard it would be to go from a life like that, to just being a normal twenty-first century woman?"

Her hand went to Grey's and squeezed it softly. "Please. Just let her stay for a few more days. Let her rest, get some distance from whatever life she left behind, and then I'll help her figure out what her next steps will be."

Grey scowled and said nothing, but I knew Seton had won, and so did she. She let out a little squeal and kissed him on the cheek. "Thank you, baby!" she grinned, and then skipped off. Before Grey could say anything, she was gone, having run upstairs to tell Cherish the good news no doubt.

"Son of a bitch," Grey said gloomily. "I can't say no to that woman."

I didn't say anything. My mind was ping-ponging back and forth between unexpected relief that I hadn't missed saying goodbye to Cherish, and unease at having to avoid her for at least another few days. I wasn't sure how the hell I was going to stand it until she was safely gone and out of my life..

CHAPTER 9

Cherish

I hadn't been sure exactly what to expect from my shopping spree with Seton, but I ended up having more fun than I could remember having in a long time. Maybe ever.

She picked me up in her car and first took me on a "grand tour of scenic Lupine," as she called it. Jokes aside, though, Lupine was a very pretty town. I hadn't seen much of it, apart from the highway into town and the bus station, so it was fun to see the different areas, from the outskirts with its small shopping centers and big box stores, to the beautiful historic main street that bustled with activity, where I had first found some members of the Stone Kings. Seton took me into the restaurant where she worked, and introduced me to her boss, a no-nonsense type woman named Jillian. Then she drove me to the house where she and Grey lived, and had me try on a few more of her clothes to see if there was anything I wanted.

"Seton," I protested. "I can't keep taking things from you. I don't have any way to pay you back."

"Yet," she interjected. "Seriously, Cherish, don't worry about it. I have more stuff than I know what to do with. Besides," she said with a twinkle in her eye. "I think that Grey and I might start trying to get pregnant sometime soon. If we do, then I won't be able to wear a lot of these clothes for long anyway."

For some reason, the mention of Seton and Grey having a baby put a picture in my head of a little infant wearing a leather jacket and covered in tattoos. I giggled to myself at the thought.

"What?" Seton asked, cocking her head.

"Nothing," I said, suppressing a grin. "Really."

She made me keep trying things on despite all of my protests. Since it seemed sort of ridiculous for me to keep running to the bathroom to change clothes, eventually I screwed up my courage and started pulling off shirts and pants in front of her. It seemed to be completely normal to her, and she barely looked at me as we continued chatting, so little by little I loosened up and forgot to feel strange about it.

One thing did catch her attention, though. "That is some kind of grandma bra," she laughed, nodding at me.

I looked down. "Is it?" I asked.

She laughed. "Cherish, it's got a ridiculous amount of material. I've seriously seen shirts that have less coverage than that. Plus, it doesn't even fit you." She hopped up from the bed where she was sitting and reached over to pinch together some of the loose fabric. "Look at that. We need to go bra shopping."

I started to protest, but then realized maybe I should just be happy that she hadn't opened a drawer and started handing me some of hers to try on. "And the same thing with those granny panties you've got on," she continued.

"What's wrong with my underwear?" I asked, confused.

"Well, for one thing, you could fit three people in there. And for another, hello, VPL."

"VPL?"

"Visible panty line." She had me turn around and showed me what she meant in the mirror. "There's just too much fabric. Trust me," she said firmly. "You'll thank me once you're wearing something that fits better and is prettier."

I started to ask her why I needed for underwear to be pretty, but my mouth shut with a pop when an image came unbidden into my mind of Levi. I imagined him looking at me in this pair of bra and panties, and suddenly, I could see what Seton meant. Not that he was ever going to see me like that, but still. If anything made me blush with more embarrassment than the thought of him seeing me naked, it was the thought of him seeing me naked with underwear that reminded him of someone's grandmother. Sighing, I agreed to let Seton take me out shopping, and hoped the experience wouldn't be too painful.

We got back into the car and headed to a shop

near one end of the main street. Before she went in, she made me swear not to look at a single price tag. "Bra shopping can be a little scary at first when you look at prices, so just don't do it. I promise that you can pay me back for the whole thing once you've settled in and gotten a job."

Seton spoke to one of the sales ladies, who introduced herself to me as Bev. Bev was very nice and immediately led me into a fitting room to measure me, then disappeared for a few minutes as I waited and tried not to feel self-conscious with the three-way mirror. She returned with a variety of bras in more colors, shapes, and styles than I had ever known existed. Mercifully, Seton let me try them on in privacy, saying only that I had to choose three, and that only one of them could be white or beige. I selected one basic one in a color Bev called nude, one light pink, and one black with a small, non-overwhelming amount of lace.

Next, we picked out enough underwear to last a week, and Seton whisked everything out of my hands and marched up to the counter to pay with a credit card. "Yay, done!" she said when she returned with the bag, which she handed to me. "Let's go get something to eat. I'm starved."

We had a late lunch at a small cafe a few doors down, watching the world go by from our table by the window as we chatted about everything and nothing. It was surprisingly easy to be around Seton, and I marveled at the fact that it seemed there were no topics that were off limits. At the Ranch, I had been so used to being careful of what I said and did, for fear of bringing shame on my family or my husband, that I hadn't really talked much about anything deeper than chores, church, or children. It felt good to have a friend I could actually say things to without worrying about being shamed for my thoughts.

Eventually, Seton started asking me more questions about where I'd come from. Once I'd answered one or two questions filling in the details of where the Ranch was, and a little about the life I'd left behind, she wanted to know how I felt about leaving the Ranch and whether I was scared of them. "Are you afraid they'll try to come find you?" she asked, her eyes wide.

"A little bit," I admitted. "Except I can't imagine how they would ever manage it. Nobody knew I was planning to leave, and I paid cash for all the bus tickets. Plus, even I didn't have any idea how to get here when I left. So I don't think they'd be able to trace my path."

She nodded, contemplating. "I suppose so. And hell, eventually they'll just have to give up, won't they? I mean, they can't force an adult to do what she doesn't want to do, so even if they find you, when you tell them you don't want to go back, they'll have to just go home and forget about it." She was silent for a moment, and then looked at me with curiosity. "And Levi really comes from there, too?"

"Yes." I tried to be careful not to give her information that Levi wouldn't want me to. "He escaped, too, when I was a little girl and he was probably seventeen or eighteen. He knew my brother Elias, and I remember hearing Elias say once afterwards that Levi had gone to a town in Colorado called Lupine. For some reason, the name stuck in my head, and when I started to get ideas about leaving, I thought that maybe if I could get here he would help me."

"Wow," she breathed. "I can't even imagine. Who would have known that Levi, of all people, was raised in a cult?" Her eyes widened in embarrassment. "Oh, I'm sorry, Cherish, I didn't mean to call it that."

"It's okay," I assured her. "I guess that's what it

might seem like, from the outside."

She looked down at her food, and after a moment looked up again, changing the subject. "What do you want to try to do for work, Cherish? Have you thought about that at all?" she asked me between bites of her salad.

"No," I admitted. "I don't really know how to do anything."

"Oh, come on, that's got to be nonsense." She waved a dismissive hand. "You told me you can cook. You must know how to do other things, as well."

"I can sew," I said. "And knit. And, um, I know how to type, actually. Other than that, not really."

"Do you know much about computers?"

"I know some," I nodded. "My first husband didn't know much about them, so I had to learn so that I could order things for the farm, things like that."

"Well, we'll figure something out," she shrugged. "Maybe you could get work waitressing at one of the restaurants in town. Or hell, there's always retail. Or working as a receptionist somewhere. We've got time."

After lunch, Seton said we had one more stop to make before we went home. Her friend and former roommate, Carly, was in town for the weekend from Denver. Carly was apparently an up and coming hair and makeup stylist who worked at a high-end salon, and when Seton had told her about me, Carly offered to give me a haircut to celebrate my freedom. We met at a small salon where Carly used to work, whose owner had given her permission to use one of the chairs for the afternoon. I was a little nervous when I met Carly and saw her artful arrangement of blond curls. "I can't wear my hair like that," I whispered to Seton. "I don't know anything about styling my hair!"

"Don't worry about it," she assured me. "She won't do anything too drastic if you don't want her to."

I took a deep breath and sat down, and an hour later, Carly had removed about three more inches and cut my hair in a way that somehow made it look lighter, fuller, and flowed around my face attractively. She even forced me to let her put on a little bit of makeup, and showed me how to do just a few tricks so that with just a little bit of mascara and a tube of something that could be used on both my cheeks and lips, I looked both just the same and completely different. I looked in the mirror and for the first time in my life, I felt beautiful.

"Thank you," I breathed. "Oh, my gosh, thank you!"

Carly beamed. "And that, my friend, is why it's on the house. Your smile is more payment than you can know."

Seton thanked Carly and hugged her goodbye, and then we drove back to the clubhouse so she could drop me off. I got back around dinnertime, but I was still full from our late lunch and too exhausted to even think about eating, so I decided to skip the meal. So much had happened that afternoon that I could hardly believe it had been less than six hours since we'd left.

Back upstairs, I put the bags down on the bed from my excursion. There was a bag of my new underwear, another bag with my clean laundry and more clothing that Seton had pressed on me, and even a small bag with a tube of mascara and another of the lip and cheek blush that Carly had given me as a present. I got to work folding and putting away the clothes that Seton had given me, chuckling softly when I found the Minions T-shirt. A few minutes later a soft knock came on the door. I opened it to see Levi standing there, his wide shoulders almost filling the doorway.

"Hey," he said softly, not quite meeting my eyes. "Can I come in for a second?"

"Of course," I said, trying to ignore the hammering in my chest. I moved away from the door and he stepped in, stopping in the middle of the living area.

When I closed the door and came to join him, he was staring at me with a look on his face I had never seen before. It was almost like he was angry, but I could tell it wasn't quite that. His entire body looked tensed, like a cat. A fierce, barely-controlled energy radiated from him, so distracting that it made me feel dizzy and almost unable to concentrate on what he was saying.

"You cut your hair," he said, his voice thick.

"I... Seton's friend cut it for me this afternoon. And put a little makeup on me," I blushed. "It's nothing, really."

"It suits you," he murmured. "All of it." His eyes

left mine to travel slowly down my body. I shivered. My skin felt as though I was in a lightning storm: every nerve seemed to be on edge, acutely aware of his electric presence.

"Thank you," I choked out.

For a moment, neither of us said anything. As his eyes traveled back up my body, they seemed to linger on every curve. A throbbing began between my legs that I recognized from the dream I had had about him. From deep down, a sort of... longing began inside me. I couldn't describe it in any other way. It was a longing so deep it was physical, but what it was I wanted, I wouldn't have been able to articulate. All I knew was that it was because of Levi, and that I wanted him to touch me.

"I came to tell you I don't mind at all that you're going to stay for a bit. I wanted to ease your mind about that," he said then. His voice, deep and rich, felt almost as though it was caressing my skin. I half-closed my eyes, my breathing growing shallow.

"I'm glad," I managed to say. "I promise I won't stay long, Levi. I know..."

"Stop!" he barked suddenly. I flinched, and he shook his head. "I'm sorry," he muttered. "I didn't mean to be yell at you. I just want you to stop worrying about how long you're going to stay." He took a half-step toward me, and I was so aware of his presence that it made me draw in my breath a little at having him so close.

"Cherish," he began, and then dropped his eyes. "What you told me earlier about why you left the Ranch. It made me realize this isn't just playing around for you. When you showed up, I was angry for the intrusion from my past. It's not a time I like to think about.

"But," he continued, "I know how hard it must have been for you to get out of there. Hell, it was hard enough for me as a man." His eyes locked on mine again, burning with intensity. "It took a lot of courage, you leaving like you did. I don't want you to feel like you have to leave until you get on your feet."

I almost started to cry with relief. My emotions were so mixed up and confused right now with Levi standing there so close to me, I didn't know how to sort out everything I was feeling, exactly, but I almost ached with the longing for him to come to me, to put his arms around me. It was so distracting I could barely think. I closed my eyes and forced myself to try and shake off the feeling. "Thank you, Levi," I said, and then laughed shakily. "It seems like all I do is thank you for things."

"Cherish," he said, his voice strange. "I want to do things for you." In the silence that followed, it felt as though the temperature in the room rose ten degrees. His green eyes were locked onto mine, seeming to reach inside me and touch parts of me I hadn't even known existed. My lips parted involuntarily, and Levi stepped slowly forward until I could feel the heat of his skin radiating toward me. The scent of leather and smoke enveloped me until I felt almost like I had after the margarita. His face towered above mine, forcing me to tilt my head back to look at him.

Levi's eyes grew dark, almost black, and he leaned forward until his face was mere inches from mine. His lips came close to my ear. "I want to do things for you," he repeated, but this time it meant something else entirely. His breath caressed my neck and the sensation almost made me gasp, it felt so intimate. Levi was touching me without laying a finger on me.

"Levi," I whispered. I was absolutely frozen to the spot, from fear mixed with so much desire that it paralyzed me. I had never wanted to be touched so badly in my life. I didn't have any idea how to react, or what to do, but I knew that if Levi kissed me or touched me in any way I might just explode. Whatever he did, I knew I would be helpless to resist anything. What was more, I realized dimly, I didn't *want* to resist. I wanted him to do something, anything. I needed, more than anything, for him relieve the terrible ache between my legs.

"Levi," I whispered again, his name a kind of plea.

He moved just a fraction of an inch closer now, until his lips were so close to my skin that if I moved at all they would be touching me. "You're fucking gorgeous, Cherish," he murmured into my ear. "It's all I can do not to take you right here." My eyes closed at the exquisite torture, my lips parted, waiting. And then, with a low groan that was almost a growl, he moved away.

I opened my eyes, confused, to find him looking down on me, almost glowering. "You can stay here as long as you want, Cherish," he said, his voice tense, almost angry. "The other men will leave you alone. But you need to stay away from me."

Then he turned and strode to the door, closing it

behind him.

I stood there, stupefied, my body fairly vibrating with need. I had no idea what had just happened. For a moment I just stood dumbly, and then all of the tensions of the past few minutes seemed to break over me like a wave. I sank to the couch and began to cry, confusion and frustration pulled out of me with every sob. I had thought Levi hated me, then that maybe he could at least tolerate me, and now... what was I to make of all that had just happened?

My sobs continued as tried to push away the image of what I had been waiting for Levi to do to me. I had never felt pleasure from a man before, but somehow I knew that what I wanted from him was for him to take me to bed, to push his hard length inside me. It was astonishing to realize that this was something a woman could want, and the fact that I had just understood it at the precise moment that Levi had decided to walk away from me was almost more than I could bear.

I didn't know if he was trying to torture me or just to warn me by being so cruel, but he could hardly have hurt me more if he'd tried. I realized that I felt more alone at this moment than I had at any point since I'd left the Ranch. Levi had warned me to stay away from him, and his cruel lesson had taught me exactly that. I didn't know how much longer I would have to stay at the Stone Kings clubhouse, but I would avoid Levi like the plague until I was able to leave.

CHAPTER 10

Levi

It had been almost two weeks since the night I almost lost control and took Cherish to bed.

Since then, we had seen each other in passing almost every day, but she would only say the most superficial greetings to me, and she refused to meet my eye.

It was exactly what I had told her she needed to do. So why did it feel like I was in some sort of self-imposed hell?

I hadn't had any intentions of anything sexual happening between us that night. Hell, I'd just gone up to the apartment to reassure her I was fine with her staying for a while. But the second she opened the door I was a goner. I didn't know why it was that every single time I saw her, she somehow got more beautiful and fucking sexier than she had been the last time. She had just returned from a day out shopping with Seton, and apparently one of Seton's friends who was a hairdresser had given Cherish a haircut. The new style was shorter, not radically different, but the cut had made her hair fuller and brought out a natural wave that made it cascade thick and full around her face. She had a little makeup on, too, just a little, and the added blush to her lips drew my eyes to them, and accentuated their fullness until I could barely look at them without imagining what they would feel like wrapped around my cock.

I thought I had steeled myself against my desire for Cherish before I walked into the apartment, but seeing her like that pretty much ambushed me, so I found myself there in the middle of the living room with a raging hard-on, with barely enough self-control to say what I had come to say and get out. I had to keep my hands fisted in my pockets to resist the urge to touch her. Even worse, it felt like she was feeling some of the same things, because her skin flushed a bit as I looked at her, her eyes dilating until I couldn't even see the pupils anymore.

My desire to fuck her senseless was just barely under control when she started to apologize again for inconveniencing me and promise up and down she wouldn't stay long. And I don't know, I just snapped a little at her. I had been thinking about what she had told me concerning her escape all day, and suddenly I couldn't stand to have her think I was mad at her for using me as a life line out of that place. So, I found myself telling her that I was glad she had come to find me, and that I admired her for having the courage to get out. In spite of all my resolve, somehow telling her that put a little crack in my armor before I even noticed it happening.

"Thank you, Levi," she said with a little laugh. "It seems like all I do is thank you for things."

Jesus, there was something about the breathy way she said my name. *Levi...* It went straight to my dick. "Cherish," I replied before I could stop myself, "I want to do things for you."

Then, fuck if I didn't move toward her and almost take her in my arms before I could stop myself. And frankly, if it had been anyone but her, I probably would have just gone for it. But it was Cherish. She had just escaped a life where sex had been something that was expected to be an unpleasant duty for women. From the way she was acting, I thought she wanted me — hell, I was almost sure of it. The way she looked at me, her lips parted like they were waiting for me to kiss her, the way her breath sped up when I got closer — her entire body was sending mine signals like a fucking beacon.

But I couldn't do it. She had to be off limits. I couldn't remember ever wanting a woman as instantly or as much as I wanted Cherish Holmes. I was pretty sure I had never wanted any woman this much in my life. Just my fucking ridiculous luck that it had to be her. But I didn't want to take advantage of someone like Cherish. I didn't want to do something that would scar her for life, even more than her husband had probably scarred her. Cherish needed time to adjust to life in the outside world. As much as I hated to admit it, I cared about her. I couldn't do something that would make it harder for her. I shouldn't even have done as much as I did. I needed to stay away from her.

That didn't mean that I was able to keep her completely out of my mind. Far from it. In the last couple of weeks, I woke up to thoughts of Cherish. I went to bed with thoughts of Cherish. I dreamed about her every goddamn night. And more times than I cared to admit, I found myself jacking off furiously to the thought of her. In the shower, or in bed, I would lean back against the tiles or the mattress and imagine pushing myself inside her hot, wet center as she wrapped her legs around me. I would stroke myself as slowly as I could to make it last, but I could never manage it for long, and soon I was coming with a loud groan, my orgasm so strong that I would see stars.

You would think that bringing myself off a few times to the image of her in my head would eventually do the trick and get my mind off of her.

You'd think fucking wrong.

Like I said, Cherish and I had exchanged little other than pleasantries in the two weeks or so since that night in the apartment. But I did manage to learn a few things about how she was progressing from what other people said. Seton and her friend Andi had managed to get Cherish an interview for a hostess position at the bar/restaurant where Andi worked, and I heard from Seton that she would be starting that job soon. I was happy for her, and broke my code of silence to stop Cherish one day as she passed by to tell her so.

"Thank you," she said simply, avoiding my eyes. "It's a relief to have a start at things."

Seton had also enlisted her brother Cal's help in giving Cherish driving lessons. Apparently, Cherish knew more or less how to drive, but hadn't done it much, so Cal took one of our cars out a few times and helped her practice. I would see them coming back together from their sessions, Cherish laughing more and more easily at Cal's flirtatious comments, and my hands would curl into angry fists. I liked Cal, and I knew I had no right to be jealous, but damned if at those moments I didn't want to push him back against the wall and pound his face in for him. I wondered if something would develop between them, and had to resist the urge to take Cal aside and tell him that Cherish was a non-starter. More than once, my stomach dropped to the floor at the realization that I might have forced myself to stay away from her, only for her to start something up with another MC brother.

One day, I was out in the garage with Frankenstein giving my bike an oil change. It was an abnormally humid day for that part of Colorado, and sweat was dripping from my forehead as I worked. As I bent over the task and tried to ignore the sting of it falling into my eyes, I heard a female voice from the other side of the bay.

"Hey, Frank," Seton called out easily. Frankenstein answered with a 'hey' back, which is more than he usually managed for anyone. Next to Frank, I pass for one loquacious motherfucker.

I looked up to see Seton approaching me. "Hey, Levi, can I ask you a favor?"

"Sure, what's up?" I asked, straightening.

"Well, I've been trying to help Cherish figure out some legal stuff, to get her started. Like, she has to fill out a W-2 for her new job at Hammie's, but in talking to her, she said she's actually not sure whether she is actually legally married to her husband."

At the mention of Cherish's name, my heart started thudding in my chest, but I kept my face a careful mask of indifference. "She doesn't know whether she's married?" I asked.

"Not really." Seton shook her head. "She said she wasn't ever legally married to her first husband —

did you know she was married once before? It's so weird! Anyway, she was, but apparently it wasn't actually an official marriage because she wasn't of legal age at the time. But she doesn't have any recollection of whether the Ranch made the second one legal." Seton looked up at me with a guarded expression. "I know you grew up there, too," she said carefully. "Would you have any idea whether marriages there are legally binding?"

A surge of anger ran through me as she spoke the words, but I tamped it down. I fucking hated anyone knowing anything about my past, but it wasn't Seton's fault. Keeping my voice neutral, I replied. "No, I don't know anything about that stuff. I left before anyone started talking about me getting married. Although," I continued, "I remember Cherish said that she was Isaiah's *second* wife." What she had told me about his first wife not liking her came back to me. "If that's the case, and he's legally married to the first one, then Cherish can't be legally married to him, too. Southern Arizona looks the other way on a lot of shit the FLDS sects do, but they still have bigamy laws."

Seton nodded as she took it all in. "Huh. Okay. Well, that's probably good news, in the grand scheme of things, but we need to know for sure, for purposes of filling out the paperwork for her job. She needs to know what her legal name is. And also," she said quietly, "I suggested that she should find out so that, if she is legally married, she should start divorce proceedings as soon as possible. So that her husband doesn't have any legal rights to anything while she's setting herself up."

I swore softly. That hadn't occurred to me. As an adult, Cherish had a legal right to come and go as she pleased, but until we knew for sure she wasn't legally bound to anyone at the Ranch, we didn't know how difficult they could make her life if they wanted to. "Yeah, good point, Seton. Thanks for thinking of that."

"No problem." She smiled. "But here's the favor I need to ask. Cherish needs to get going on this stuff, and she needs to go over to the county courthouse and make a request to look up a marriage license, and also to see if she has a social security number. It being Thursday, she should try to get the requests filled out before the weekend, but I have to go to work soon, so I can't take her. Could you?"

It was the last goddamn thing in the world I wanted to do. It was on the tip of my tongue to ask Seton if she could find someone else to take Cherish, but then the thought of her asking Cal to do it stopped me. Cursing myself for being such a jealous bastard, I said, "Sure. I can do it. When does she want to go?"

Seton smiled. "Thanks, Levi! You're the best. I think she's ready to go any time, actually. You want me to let her know?"

I sighed. "Yeah, I'll just finish up here and clean up. Have her come down in about half an hour."

Fuck.

Cherish came into the garage a while later wearing a simple blue-and-white striped camisole top, cut off jean shorts and flip flops. It was the first time I'd ever seen her wearing shorts, and the sight of her legs, which I'd imagined wrapped around me so many times in my fantasies, was almost more than I could take.

I had worked myself into a piss-poor mood anyway at the thought of having to spend the next couple of hours with her, and unfortunately I was on edge enough that I wasn't able to keep myself from lashing out at her.

"You can't wear those goddamn flip flops on the bike," I growled at her, nodding toward her sandals. "Go change into some other shoes."

Startled, she looked down, then back up at me. "We're taking your motorcycle?" she asked.

"What the hell else did you think we were gonna take?" I barked.

Her surprise shifted to anger at my harsh words. "Okay, you don't need to bite my head off," she retorted. "I'll go change." She turned in a huff and marched back toward the clubhouse without another word. Unfortunately, her going to change meant that I had to watch her ass as she retreated. I ran through every swear word I could think of as I went to wash off my hands and splash cold water over my face.

She came back a few minutes later wearing a pair of tennis shoes, her jaw set angrily. She avoided my eyes as I handed her my helmet and showed her how to put it on. When I reached forward to help her attach it under her chin, she pulled back. "I can do it," she muttered. I watched her in irritated silence as she fumbled clumsily with the straps until she finally managed to snap them together.

I straddled the bike and motioned with my head

for her to get on. She paused for a moment, obviously reluctant, and I resisted the urge to bark at her. Above and beyond this being her first time on a motorcycle, I knew she had rarely had physical contact with a member of the opposite sex. Finally, after a few moments, she awkwardly got on behind me.

"Put your feet on those pedals there," I instructed, "and wrap your arms around me." Again, she hesitated, and I waited until she tentatively did as I told her. My chest tightened at the feel of her pressed up against me, but I fought it off and continued. "When we turn, the bike's gonna lean. You want to lean into the turn with me, not against it. That's important. Just follow my lead. Think you can do that?"

I felt her nod. "Yes."

"Good." I started up the bike, and we were off. As soon as I put the bike in gear and we began to move forward, Cherish's arms tightened around me in fear. I made sure to drive as smoothly as I could, with no sudden moves, and after a couple of minutes I could feel her relax a bit. I took the first few turns slowly, to give her time to get used to the bike leaning, and to her credit, it didn't take her long to get the hang of it. By the time we arrived at the county courthouse, I could tell her body had relaxed almost completely. I was impressed.

Pulling into a parking space toward the front of the building, I cut the engine and told Cherish to get off first. When she removed her helmet, I saw that she was smiling. "That was fun," she said, giving me a sheepish grin.

It was sort of cute that her mood had changed so quickly just from a short ride, and I felt my irritation at her begin to melt away. "Glad you liked it," I said in a tone that didn't come out as gruff as I wanted it to.

We headed into the courthouse, which luckily also had a Social Security Administration office, so we went there first. Cherish gave her full name and date of birth to the woman behind the counter. I realized that her twenty-second birthday would be in just a few weeks, and that, like anyone who had grown up in the WFZ community, she had probably never celebrated it. I wasn't big on birthdays myself, but remembering that made me kind of sad for her, anyway.

Unfortunately, it turned out that Cherish had never been issued a social security number. In order to get one, the office was asking for the original of her birth certificate and a second form of ID like a driver's license, neither of which Cherish had. The woman behind the counter suggested that Cherish could bring in an employee ID card or a school ID instead of the license, but she didn't have those, either. After a few minutes of going around and around with the woman behind the counter, it was clear that Cherish's first encounter with government bureaucracy was taking its toll on her. She walked out of that office in a daze, looking up at me with a bewildered expression.

"What am I going to do, Levi? If I can't get a social security number, they won't let me work!" Her eyes were bright with unshed tears.

Smiling at Cherish reassuringly, I said, "Don't worry about it. You must have a birth certificate, so you just have to apply to get an original sent to you."

"What about the second form of ID?"

I thought back to my own escape years ago. I had been lucky; I'd been able to get a driver's license before I left. Unfortunately, you needed a residential address for that, too. I furrowed my brow, lost in thought for a moment, and then remembered that the club had a contact who specialized in creation of realistic identification documents. Chico could easily mock up a driver's license for Cherish, but in this case, she would need a real one eventually, anyway. Better to have him do something simple, like the school ID. That would be enough to get her going on the social security number, and she wouldn't have to wait until she'd passed her driver's license.

"Look, don't worry," I said calmly. "The club has it covered. We just need to stop at the passport office downstairs and take some ID photos on the way out. There's a photo booth down there. It'll just take a few minutes."

Next, we followed the signs to the office that dealt with marital and divorce records. Here, the process for getting information was a lot simpler. It turned out all we had to do was provide the names of the bride and groom, the county where the marriage license would have been issued, and the date of the wedding. However, since Cherish had been married — if she was married — in Arizona, she needed to contact the courthouse of the county where the Ranch was located.

Cherish was kind of dispirited as left the courthouse. "We didn't get anything done that we wanted to do," she said gloomily as we descended the stairs.

"Sure we did," I argued. "We got a lot of information. And we got your ID photos taken care of," I said, nodding toward the small envelope she carried.

"What good will those do?" she shrugged.

"Look, most offices don't look very hard at identification cards. It's not that difficult to make one that looks convincing."

Cherish's eyes widened. "You mean lie?" she asked.

I grinned. "I mean, give them what they want. Cherish, making up a school ID card isn't going to send you to jail. Or to Hell."

She went quiet at that, and I didn't push it. We continued out into the parking lot, and she wordlessly took the helmet I offered her. She seemed so disappointed by everything that my mind was casting about trying to think of ways to cheer her up. Suddenly, it was obvious.

"Hey, let's take a ride," I suggested. "Out of town. Take a break from thinking about all this stuff."

Cherish looked at the bike, and then at me. A slow smile spread across her face. "That sounds like a great idea," she said. My heart surged as she beamed up at me. I had never seen her look as radiant as now, at the simple pleasure of a ride on my bike, and suddenly all I ever wanted to do in the world was find things to do for her that would make her look at me like that forever.

CHAPTER 11

Cherish

We rode out of town in the late afternoon, and the traffic was pretty light. I felt more comfortable on the bike now, and I could feel that Levi was taking the turns a little faster, but never so much that I was afraid.

It was such a beautiful day, and being on such a powerful machine was a thrill like none I'd ever experienced before. It was amazing to feel the wind on my skin, and to be able to smell the fresh, clean scent of pines as we flew by them. I understood now why people rode motorcycles. Being here with Levi, I felt more alive, more aware of everything around me, than I had ever felt before.

Of course, there was also the fact that I was pressed against Levi's muscular back, my arms around his taut waist. When he first motioned to me to get onto the bike back at the clubhouse, I would rather have had the earth open up and swallow me than do what he said. But seeing as I had no choice if I wanted to get the documents I needed to start my new job, I swallowed my embarrassment and did as I was told. The slope of the seat meant that I could hardly avoid being pushed up against him. I was sure my face was red as a beet as I realized I had to wrap my arms around him or risk falling off the motorcycle. I had never been so nervous in my whole life, not even on my wedding night with Isaiah.

The roar of the engine underneath us wasn't a surprise, though it was louder up close. What was a surprise, though, was that I could feel it between my legs, and every time that Levi boosted the throttle, it sent shivers of response through my body. As he leaned us through the turns, my thighs instinctively pressed together trying to hold on, but instead of gripping the seat, they found Levi's muscular thighs. I felt them flex as he worked the pedals, and a rush of heat flooded through me, pooling below my stomach. It had been hard enough to try to ignore my desire for him at the clubhouse the last several days, when I could scurry for my room whenever he appeared. Now, wrapped around him on the back of his bike, my senses were flooded with him. I felt almost dizzy with need, and yet all I could do was hold on and hope he couldn't sense the tumult inside me.

We headed east for so long that I lost track of time and finally gave in to the guilty pleasure of Levi's presence and heat against my body. Eventually, he slowed to a stop at a mesa with a breathtaking view of a valley below. I got off the bike and took off my helmet, my mouth widening in surprise at the beauty of it.

"Ooohh," I breathed. "Levi, it's amazing."

He grinned at me. "I thought you might like it." He headed for a large table-top rock on the edge of the mesa, and I followed and lowered myself down next to him.

We sat for a few minutes in silence, just enjoying

the magnificent view and the stillness of it all. There was just enough of a breeze to make it comfortable, and I closed my eyes and told myself to remember that if I hadn't left the Ranch, I never would have seen this.

Levi's voice interrupted my thoughts. "You feeling a little better now?"

"Yes. Much. Thank you," I replied, opening my eyes to look at him. His expression was warmer than it usually was, and it stirred something inside me that made me look away toward the valley. "I'm sorry I got upset at the courthouse. Sometimes I feel like maybe I'm not strong enough to make it in the outside world," I confessed to him. "It's just so overwhelming sometimes. Like all this paperwork I don't have, and I have no idea how to get it. It's like everything is telling me I don't belong."

He nodded. "I remember. When I left the WFZ, I realized I didn't know how to do a fucking thing in the real world." He glanced at me apologetically. "Sorry. I didn't mean to swear."

"It's okay," I reassured him. "Honestly, I think over the years, I've started to realize that words are just words. I've learned from experience that people can say the nicest words you've ever heard, but poison can still be dripping from them."

He chuckled. "You're not kidding." We sat companionably for a few moments, lost in our own thoughts, until Levi finally turned to me with a long, penetrating look. "You know, what you told me about why you decided to escape? The final straw that made you decide," he said slowly. "Did you ever hear anything at the Ranch about why I left?"

"No," I replied. "Like I said before, you're shunned. Hardly anyone ever talked about you, and then only in whispers. And don't forget, I was just a little girl when it all happened. Even if they were talking about it at the time, it wasn't to me."

Levi reached into his pocket and took out a cigarette. Lighting it, he blew out a long plume of smoke and sighed heavily. "I had a little sister. Faith. From the sounds of it, she wasn't much older than the stepdaughter you mentioned having. The one who's about to be married. My father married Faith off to one of the elders when she was fourteen, and she got pregnant pretty soon after that.

"When she was pretty far along — at least seven months, I'd say — she showed up at our house one night. She was crying, and her face was all bloodied and bruised. Turned out, *he* had beaten her up, because she was afraid to have sex with him that late into the pregnancy." I turned to see Levi's face contorted in suppressed rage. "Instead of helping her — instead of fucking *doing* something — my father sent her back to him." He looked at me with murder in his eyes. "Her husband beat her again a few weeks later for the same reason. She lost the baby and bled to death because he didn't call anybody to help her."

"Levi!" I whispered in horror. "My God."

His face was grim as he continued, determined to finish the story. "I went after Faith's husband with a two by four. Broke a couple of bones in his face before I was through. And when my father found out, he beat the shit out of me for doing it. So I left."

I sat, paralyzed, watching the muscles in Levi's jaw work as he fought to control himself. His anger was so raw, so close to the surface, I realized it had probably taken him years to push all of it down out of sight. No wonder he hated the idea of anyone knowing about his past. And when I arrived at the clubhouse that day, I had brought everything back. I was a reminder of everything he had tried to put behind him, just by being here.

Suddenly I hated myself for what I'd done. I'd been so selfish to just assume that it would be easy enough for Levi to take me in, that the only thing I would be asking of him was some lodging and maybe some direction. I never realized that I could be opening up old wounds that had barely healed. "Levi... I don't know what to say. I can't believe my coming here has brought all this back to you." I looked at him as my eyes pricked with regretful tears. "I wish I'd never tried to find you. I was so selfish, and cowardly. I should never have forced you to help me."

"Cherish," he frowned. His eyes met mine, and where they had been stormy, now they softened. "Don't. Don't do that." He reached up, and with a softness that astonished me, brushed a tear carefully from my cheek with his thumb. I drew in my breath, his touch electric against my skin.

"I'm glad you came," he murmured. "I'm glad that knowing there was someone out there who might help you got you to leave. And, don't say you're a coward." He looked at me fiercely. "It took you far more courage to leave than it took me. I'm a man. Even as hard as it was for me to leave everything I knew and go out into the world, it was nothing compared to the risk you took in coming here. Jesus, you could have been…" Abruptly, he stopped.

"What?" I asked him.

Then, before I knew what was happening, his mouth came down on mine. Everything I thought I understood about what it was like to be kissed flew away under his touch. His mouth and tongue were warm and insistent, his lips so soft, that as his mouth teased mine open it felt like I was turning to melting lava. Dizzily, I felt his arms go around me, pulling me to him, and without thinking, my lips and tongue began to answer his. One hand moved up from my lower back, twining in my hair, and his kiss deepened as he held me to him.

Levi pulled away a little, his dark eyes penetrating mine. I was gasping for breath, my lips parted. I was afraid to beg him, but desperate for him to kiss me again.

"Tell me if you want me to stop," he demanded, his voice low and urgent.

"I don't want you to stop," I whispered.

With an almost animal growl, his mouth found mine again. His kiss grew deeper, more demanding, and I opened to him. The hot throb between my legs, which I had felt so often lately when thinking of him, began deep inside me and grew almost painful. I was desperate for something I barely understood, but I instinctively knew that Levi could take me there. His mouth left mine and slowly began to trace a trail down my neck. I had no idea that a simple touch could feel like that.

A loud moan escaped my lips, and my eyes flew open with embarrassment. My body must have tensed, because Levi chuckled deep in his throat. "Don't be embarrassed, Cherish," he murmured against my skin. "That's the hottest damn sound I've ever heard."

He continued to brush his lips down my neck, his tongue flicking against the soft spot at the base of my throat. My nipples tightened in response, and I arched my back, suddenly knowing that what I wanted was to have his mouth there. As if Levi had read my mind, I felt one of his hands reach to the bottom of my shirt and gently begin to push it up over my stomach. My breath caught in my throat and I resisted the urge to stop him, knowing that it was only my upbringing that made me feel that I should. The fact was, every cell in my body was crying out for him, and I knew that whatever happened, the only thing I wanted was for him to keep touching me and not stop.

His hand gently caressed the sensitive skin on my stomach, before sliding back to the clasp of my bra. Crazily, I almost laughed, and sent a silent thanks to Seton for making me go underwear shopping. I shivered as I felt the fabric loosen, my breasts heavy and fully, waiting for his touch. Levi gently lowered me onto my back on the flat rock, and I held my breath and shut my eyes in anticipation, then gasped as I felt his lips find my right nipple.

Again, I felt my back arch, this time knowing it was because my body was asking him for more. I moaned again, straining toward him, as his tongue began to lick and lap at the hard nub. The ache between my legs grew, and throbbed; I felt stretched tight as a rubber band. My muscles were taut, and tense, straining toward something I needed so badly that everything else had fallen away. His lips left one nipple, and then grazed my skin before finding the other. The pleasure was agony, and I was almost crying with it. He held me like that, teasing first one bud and then the other, until I was whispering, "Please!" over and over, without even knowing what exactly I was begging him for.

One hand gently began to touch the skin on my inner thigh, light as a feather, and I felt it slide slowly toward the place in me that felt like the center of all my need. His touch was light, so light that I could barely stand it, and then he had found my core, and I could feel that I was wet, soaking even, and as he touched me, I was coating his fingers with my desire. Softly, he began to stroke me there, my wetness making his finger slick against my skin. I cried out, my legs spreading wide in spite of myself. I knew exactly where the core of all this desire was, then, I could feel it, and suddenly I could feel exactly where I wanted him to touch me, more than anything on the earth. My hips thrust toward his hand impatiently, and he chuckled in appreciation. "Cherish, you have no idea how beautiful you are."

He teased me a bit, drawing back as I strained forward, clearly enjoying my frustration. Finally, when I thought I would go crazy from the agony, he leaned up and kissed me deeply, and at last swirled around the slick center of my desperate torment. Before I knew what was happening, I exploded.

The world and everything in it felt like it had shattered into a billion pieces. I could hear myself calling Levi's name, but I had no sense of myself doing it. It was as though he had torn his name from my throat, drawn everything in me inside out with this white-hot heat. I felt myself rock and shudder, and then his arms were around me, holding me as I continued to quiver and shake. When finally I slowed, barely able to catch my breath, I opened my eyes to find Levi staring at me, his eyes as dark as I'd ever seen them.

"That was fucking gorgeous," he murmured. "Excuse my French."

I laughed softly as his lips dipped to mine for a gentle kiss. I was so exhausted I could barely return it.

We stayed like that, talking quietly together, until the sun began its slow descent toward the horizon. It was strange; I couldn't member ever feeling more content, or more protected, safe in the arms of this dangerous bad boy biker with his tough shell of tattoos. He had given me a glimpse of the softer side of him, a door into his past that he took great care to keep tightly closed off from others.

I didn't have any idea what the future held. Most of it scared the life out of me. To be honest, what had just happened between Levi and me scared the life out of me, in a way. But right then, right there, I was happy being in the arms of this dark, dangerous man. And, I decided, I needed to be thankful for that moment of uncomplicated bliss, no matter what happened, or where I found myself tomorrow.

CHAPTER 12

Levi

The day after I took Cherish to the mesa and made love to her, I hardly knew what the fuck to do with myself.

Feeling her respond under me as I kissed her, pushing away the fabric of her shorts and finding her so wet and ready for me… Seeing her face as she came with utter abandon… Jesus, the only word I could find for what it made me feel was *joy*. She was so beautiful, and she trusted me so completely as I touched her in ways I was sure she'd never been touched before. No, it was obvious that all of this was new to her. It made me both angry that no man had ever cared enough about her pleasure to pay attention to her like that, and bursting with pride and something else I couldn't even name that I had been the one to wake her body for the first time. For once, it didn't matter at all that I'd been dying to possess her, to find my own release, to feel her hot pussy throb around my cock as I came. I was rock hard the whole time, and I knew I was in for a world class case of blue balls, but I didn't care. Right then, what mattered was Cherish, and I wanted everything to be about her.

After I had driven her back to the clubhouse and kissed her goodnight outside the door of the apartment, I drove back to my place in a kind of drunken stupor. It was almost like I didn't recognize myself. I couldn't ever remember feeling even remotely like this about another woman. The fact that it was someone so inexperienced and innocent about the world was even more confusing. Not that Cherish was a cold fish; far from it. I could tell just by the way her body responded, by the sensual moans that escaped from deep in her throat, that she was a highly sexual woman. It was only a matter of time before she learned how to give as good as she got. And I wanted to be the man who was there for it. For once, the idea of going slow, of taking my time with a woman, seemed more appealing than just getting my rocks off and moving on to the next thing. I got back to my place, went straight to the bathroom, and jumped into the hottest shower I could stand, stroking myself to a shuddering release at the memory of Cherish coming under my hand.

The following day, I was having a hell of a time thinking about anything but her. I found myself eagerly anticipating seeing her as my bike ate up the road between my place and the clubhouse. I felt like a goddamn schoolboy, and I didn't know whether to be disgusted with myself or just run with it. When I got there, Cherish was already up and about and in the kitchen, making a large breakfast of bacon and eggs that must have been for some of the brothers. Her hair was tied up in a loose pony. She was wearing a green sundress that I hadn't seen before, and it showed off her legs and made me want to slip my hands under it and have my way with her.

"Hello, gorgeous," I said into her ear as I slipped my arms around her from behind.

Cherish leaned back against me and looked up.

Her eyes were shining. "Hey, you," she answered.

I turned her around gently and gave her a deep kiss as I drew her to me. She pressed eagerly against me, whimpering softly.

"No kissing the cook when she's makin' my breakfast," Trig growled loudly from the doorway. I looked up to see him mock-frowning at me with a curious glint in his eye. "Don't come between me and my food, Wolff."

"I wouldn't think of it," I said easily. "There enough for me, Sunshine?" I asked the beautiful girl in my arms.

"There's enough for everybody who wants some." Her smile was just for me, and it made my heart leap in my chest.

"Well, ain't this a picture of domestic bliss," Moose, our Enforcer, announced, as he brushed past Trig and headed for a seat at the kitchen table. "Coffee ready?"

"There's a full pot, just waiting for you," Cherish told him as she turned back to the skillet she was stirring. My arms were still around her, and Moose eyed me curiously for a moment, then grunted and grabbed a mug out of the cupboard.

"What's on your agenda for today?" I asked her as I watched her flip the bacon.

"I have to call the county courthouse in Arizona to find out about whether I'm legally married, and then call the licensing bureau to find out whether I need an appointment to take my driving test. After that, I'm going into town to stop by Hammie's and give my new boss an update on how getting my official documents is going. Depending on what they say when I call the courthouse, I may go make an appointment to talk to a divorce lawyer."

I marveled at how calmly she said the last bit. So much was new to her, and she had to be terrified at the prospect of initiating proceedings against Isaiah Whitehead, but she wasn't letting any stress she felt show. I squeezed her tight and murmured into her ear, "Whatever you need me to do for you, you let me know."

"Thank you, Levi. Actually," she blushed, "I guess you could ask your friend to make me that fake school ID card."

I grinned. "Done." I'd call my man Lefty right after breakfast. "How are you getting into town?"

"Walking," she shrugged.

"That's over three miles," I told her.

"I know," she grinned. "I walked it the first day, when I came from there to here, remember? Don't worry, I'm not gonna break."

"There's no sidewalk for most of it. You shouldn't be walking along that road."

"Well, that's why I need to get my license. And eventually a car," she said mildly. "Don't worry about it, Levi. I'll be completely fine. I actually like walking. It'll be good to get some exercise."

I grumbled a response and made a note to take her in myself, later. For now, the club had church in a few minutes.

The men were in a more jovial mood than usual as Grey banged the gavel, which I attributed to the effects of Cherish's delicious breakfast. Apart from the usual business, the main topic of discussion was some vandalism that had occurred to some of the equipment and vehicles outside our garage. As the discussion progressed, the mood worsened, and tension became palpable.

"Anything on the security cams?" Repo asked.

"Too dark," Grey commented. "Saw a few figures, but nothing much to identify them. All we know is there were three of them, and looks like they showed up around 3:18 in the morning. They were gone within ten minutes."

"Goddamnit," raged Winger. "I am fucking sick of sitting around and doing nothing about this Cannibals problem. We're acting like a bunch of fucking pussies. I say we go over there and knock enough skulls together to make them think more than twice about coming back here again."

"We still don't know for sure who it is," Cal pointed out. "Shit, the vandalism could have been high school kids, for all we know."

"This is what I'm talking about, acting like a bunch of fucking frightened little pieces of shit!" Winger roared back. "What the hell, Cal, do you seriously think some goddamn high school kids would have the balls to come to the Stone Kings clubhouse just to slash a few tires? This ain't kids, brother. This is the Cannibals, doing shit to make us look even weaker when we don't retaliate."

"Seems to me the pussies are the goddamn Cannibals, if they're too scared to put a signature on what they're doing." Cal replied.

"If it is them. Which we still don't know for sure," Grey said quietly. Some of the men grumbled, and from the sound of it, the ones that were grumbling were getting sick of waiting for a clear sign before we made a move. Grey had a long, slow burn, and I respected him for that. But the men were starting to get antsy, out of a desire for vengeance. Hell, even I was starting to think doing anything was better than doing nothing at all.

"Fuck it," Trig interjected. "This shit has got to stop." His voice rose as his fist pounded once on the table for emphasis. "I don't care if it's risky with the cartel. We need to act. The longer we sit around and try to figure out for sure who's attacking us, the weaker we look. And the weaker we look, the weaker we become."

I opened my mouth to respond, when the room concussed, a sudden boom and then a whoosh of the air that seemed to take all sound with it. Then, into the sound vacuum came the noise of shattering glass, but muted, as if impossibly far away. My ears felt as though the drums had been pushed in, and the outer chamber filled with cotton. Hard, pelting rain came down on my back and arms, biting into my skin like a thousand tiny insect stings.

Dazed, I was unable to move for a few moments as my lizard brain tried to get some sort of bead on what had just happened. I had flung myself to the floor instinctively, and now I cautiously took my arms away from my head, ready to get back into position if a second blast came. I opened my eyes and looked up to see dust everywhere, filling the shafts of sunlight coming through the broken windows like impossibly small snowflakes. I started coughing, violently, but the sound coming from my own throat sounded like it came from the other side of the clubhouse. In between coughing fits I called to my brothers, but couldn't hear if they answered. Eventually the dust began to clear enough for me to see some of the others as they struggled to stand up. I looked wildly around the room as one by one, my brothers appeared, dusty and confused, through the haze.

Head pounding, ears still ringing, I staggered to my feet and lunged for the door. *Cherish.* Out in the clubhouse, men and women looked around in confusion as they tried to process what had just happened. I knew in my gut that this was the Cannibals, but right now I didn't care. The only thing that mattered right now was Cherish. I had to find her, had to know she was okay.

I stumbled toward the kitchen where I'd last seen her, but there was no one there. Turning, I raced up the stairs to her apartment, not bothering to knock. The door wasn't locked, and I burst inside to find it empty. Wildly, I ran back downstairs, but I could find no sign of her.

Back in the main room of the clubhouse, I could see many people who looked to have minor injuries and cuts, but at first glance, no one seemed seriously hurt. My hearing was beginning to improve a little, and I stopped a few people and asked them if they'd seen Cherish. One of the women said she had left some time ago, and relief flooded my veins, making me feel light-headed. I rushed back to the chapel, where my brothers were all standing now, looking around at the damage and shouting directions at one another.

"Everyone seems okay outside," I told Grey. I yelled over to our resident medical man. "Patch, you good?"

"Yeah," he shouted back. "I'll grab some supplies and get to work patching people up."

A few of us went outside to survey the damage. Apart from some blown-out windows on the east side and some wall damage on that side as well, the main part of the building looked to be largely intact with no structural damage evident.

"Winger," Grey barked. "Grab the surveillance video from this morning. There's no way they'll get away without a trace this time."

"Grey." Trigger was standing in front of us now, his hair covered in dust. "Do we need to go on lockdown?"

I watched our president consider this. On the one hand, we needed to get all the Stone Kings and their families in one place to know they were safe. On the other, given the clubhouse had just been targeted, was this the safest place to have them?

His brow furrowed, and he made the decision. "Have the men do a thorough check of the perimeter, inside and out. Once they're sure there's nothing more on the premises, call a lockdown. We're gonna get the people who did this," Grey seethed, turning to me. The fire in his eyes burned bright and unforgiving. "And they are gonna pay. I don't care what it costs."

I needed to find Cherish, and bring her back before the lockdown started. I told Grey where I was going and jumped on my bike, flying into town on the route I knew she must have taken. I found her just as she was emerging from the courthouse. Her hand flew to her mouth as she saw me. I must have looked like hell from the expression on her face.

"Levi, what happened?" she cried.

"Get on," I yelled at her. "Don't ask questions. I'll tell you back at the clubhouse."

CHAPTER 13

Cherish

It was really, really awkward getting on Levi's bike in my sundress, but the look on his face told me in no uncertain terms that I needed to just do as he said and not ask him why.

When we got back to the clubhouse and I saw the damage, I let out a shocked cry of alarm. A couple dozen Stone Kings, some covered in dust, were milling around, barking orders at each other and scanning the scene with sharp eyes. I saw guns tucked into back waistbands, and a few of the men speaking into two-way radios in low voices.

Scrambling off the bike as gracefully as I could, I handed my helmet to Levi and finally tried to ask the question that had been in my mind since he came to get me. "What happened to —?"

"Upstairs," he roared at me, making me jump. My eyes widened in surprise as I stalked mutely toward the stairwell, then up to the apartment. He followed me through the door, then slammed it with a loud bang.

"Goddamnit!" he shouted.

I flinched. I'd never seen Levi behave like this, and I couldn't figure out why he was so angry with me all of a sudden. "Why are you yelling?" I cried.

"I'm not yelling!" he yelled. "Jesus!" He began to pace back and forth, running a hand through his hair.

Okay, now I was just getting mad on top of being scared. "Levi. Stop it." My voice was sharp. "You have got to tell me what's going on."

"Where were you?" he demanded, his voice

thundering through the apartment. He stopped his pacing and stood in front of me, a challenge in his eyes.

"You know very well where I was!" My hands went to my hips as I confronted him. "I told you earlier where I was going, and that's where I went!"

"You could have…" he cut himself off, then pointed a finger at me. "Don't just go off on your own again. What if something had happened to you? How the hell was anyone supposed to get in touch with you?"

I scowled at him and reached into the pocket of my dress. "Seton gave me a burner phone," I told him, thrusting it in his face. "She put her number in it, in case I needed to get hold of her."

Levi's eyes widened as they fixed on the phone I held in my hand. He seemed slightly mollified, but he wasn't ready to give up his anger just yet.

"Why didn't you give me the number?" he demanded.

I sighed at him in annoyance. "Levi. You were in a meeting when I left. What was I supposed to do, burst in there and interrupt you?"

His hand went back to his hair, running roughly through it. He was quiet for a moment, then let out a long groan. Shutting his eyes, he fell into the low chair behind him.

"Goddamn…" he muttered. "Goddamn."

"Levi." I sat down on the edge of the coffee table in front of him. "What is going on? Will you please stop for a minute, and explain what happened, and why you're so angry with me?"

He sighed and opened his eyes. "I'm not angry with you, Cherish. I'm just… I was just worried."

My heart began to hammer with emotion. He was worried about me. Why did that make me feel so… happy? I had to push down the thrill that his words had caused inside me. "Worried *why*, Levi?" I nodded toward the door. "Tell me what happened out there."

"An explosion," he said tiredly leaning back in the chair. "Someone bombed the club."

My eyes widened in horror. "Was anyone hurt?"

"I don't think so. Minor cuts and stuff, from what I can tell."

I looked at his arms and noticed the nicks and scratches for the first time. "You're bleeding."

He shook his head. "It's nothing."

"Levi," I said softly. "I'm fine. Nothing happened to me. Let's stop this arguing and focus on going down there and helping people clean up."

He looked up at me, a raw fierceness in his eyes that I should have been afraid of, but wasn't. He came out of the chair and then he was kneeling in front of me. He was so tall that his eyes were level with mine. Taking me in his arms, he kissed me, his lips hard and demanding. I moaned against his mouth as the now-familiar heat I felt at his touch flooded through me.

Levi picked me up in his arms and carried me to the bed. He lay me down, then moved over me, his body pressing me down into the mattress. I could feel his hardness pressing against my hot core, and I gasped and felt my body angle up of its own accord to meet him. *Oh…* It felt almost unimaginably good, this communication of our bodies, and suddenly all I could think about was wanting nothing between us. No fabric, nothing but flesh on flesh. A plea died in my throat as he kissed me again, his tongue probing, insisting. His beard scratched the soft skin of my face, and I marveled at how much I loved the sensation. I wanted to feel him, all of him, everything…

His mouth broke from mine and his lips grazed my ear. "Cherish, I want you, so badly," he whispered. "I can't think about anything but you. You're driving me crazy."

Every nerve ending in my body was crying out for his touch. "Levi… please…"

"Tell me, Cherish," he murmured against my throat. "You have to tell me what you want. I won't go further than you're ready for."

"Levi," I whispered. "Please… take me."

He raised his head to look at me. His eyes were dark like the night. "Cherish. Are you sure?"

"Yes," I breathed. "Yes."

Levi raised himself up and knelt over me. Reaching behind himself, he pulled off his T-shirt in one fluid motion, revealing a mosaic of intricate tattoos that covered his arms, chest, and stomach. My mouth opened in wonder at the way they moved as his muscles flexed. I reached a tentative hand out to touch his stomach, marveling at the taut firmness of his skin. Levi shuddered slightly as my fingers traveled across his abdomen.

"Jesus, Cherish," he groaned. "I don't know how you do this to me."

Below his waistline, the outline of his erection strained against his jeans. The throb between my legs grew as I imagined him entering me. With more courage than I knew I possessed, I let my fingers trail southward until they grazed the hard length of him through the fabric. He inhaled sharply, watching me touch him with eyes that burned with desire.

My lips parted as my hand closed over his length. I felt him pulsing against my touch, and I drew in my breath, knowing that he was pulsing for me. The thought came unbidden that I wanted to taste him, to explore his manhood with my tongue, as I had never done before with any man. I blushed furiously, knowing he couldn't read my mind but feeling shy for thinking it just the same.

I began to stroke him through his jeans, instinctively understanding this would feel good to him, and he groaned loudly and closed his hand over mine. "Wait," he said simply. "I won't last long like that. You've got me too wound up."

He lay back down, covering me with his body, and began kissing me again, deeply. His hand traveled to my thigh, and began to lightly stroke the soft inner skin. I moaned softly as I remembered what he had done to me the first time he'd touched me. My legs parted, and his stroking continued. Slowly, he pushed my dress up as got nearer to my pulsing center. A finger, then two, slipped underneath my panties, finding my soaking core, and he began to stroke me there, first softly, then more insistently. He chuckled in satisfaction as I gasped and arched toward his touch, my hand clutching desperately at his arm. After a few moments he withdrew, and slowly brought his finger to his mouth, sucking my juices from his skin as his eyes bored deep into mine.

He sat up again, and pulled my dress up past my hips. Wordlessly, I overcame my embarrassment and raised my arms for him to slip it over my head. He tossed it to the floor, then sat back to look at me. I forced myself not to shy away from his gaze. "You're so fucking gorgeous, Cherish," he breathed, shaking his head. He reached out a hand and cupped one of my breasts, teasing my nipple to hardness through my bra. Heat coursed through me, making the ache between my legs stronger, almost unbearable now. He reached behind me and unclasped the bra, pulling it off and throwing it next to my dress. As I waited, his eyes traveled over my body slowly, taking in the fullness of my breasts and the heated flush of my skin. Levi drew in his breath and let it out with a low growl, then lay me back on the bed and began to tease one nipple with his tongue as he continued to softly pinch the other with his thumb and forefinger.

I lay there, my body quivering with the sweet agony, marveling at how it could feel so wonderful and so torturous at the same time. I remembered how he had made me orgasm last time, and what he was doing to me now was so intense I thought I might come like that if he didn't stop. It felt like I was riding a wave that was pushing me higher and higher, and all I could think about was getting to the top and going over. I was desperate for him to take me there, could barely wait for him to give me what I needed so badly, now that I knew how amazing it could be.

Levi's mouth left my breast and seared a burning path down my stomach. Between my legs, my nub began to throb almost painfully. He went slowly, kissing and tasting my skin as he went, and when he moved below my belly button I suddenly realized where he was going. I gasped and started to sit up, but he gently pushed me down with one hand. My eyes were wide as I stared at the ceiling in apprehension. It was too much; I couldn't let him do something so... intimate. I started to push him away weakly with my hands, but my body was already betraying me. The ache between my legs wanted his touch so badly, that when he reached to pull down my panties, I raised my hips to help him, unable to resist any longer. He spread my legs and knelt between them. My breathing was coming fast and shallow now, and I froze as I waited in terror and anticipation.

At the first hot, slick lap of his tongue against my needy nub, I gasped and cried out in pleasure. Nothing, nothing could ever have prepared me for the sweetness of this. Oh, God, the agony! From the second he began, I was unhinged. I writhed, I bucked against him, I called his name. He licked, and sucked, and lapped at me, giving me at once everything and not nearly enough with each flick of his expert tongue. Everything fell away, all my shyness, all my apprehension, as I gave myself to him, letting him tease me and lead me, bringing me close to the edge, and then backing away, only to bring me even higher. My hands fisted in his hair, my hips arched and thrusted to meet his touch. He licked and suckled me until finally I was begging him to release me. Then, with a deep, satisfied rumble in his throat, he drew me between his lips and licked me one more time, and I flew over the edge, calling his name as I shuddered and bucked against his tongue.

I was gasping for breath as I heard Levi unzip and remove his pants. I heard the rip of a plastic wrapper, and then he was leaning over me, looking deep into my eyes. "I know this isn't your first time," he murmured. "But tell me if you need me to stop." I nodded, returning his gaze without a word. Then the hot, hard skin of his length was pressing against my still throbbing center. My lips parted in pleasure as I spread my legs to take him all in.

Levi began to push inside me, slowly at first, his eyes closed in concentration. He withdrew, then pushed in again, farther, and it was so good that I threw my head back and moaned. Finally, after the third thrust, he was inside me all the way. He froze for a moment, then opened his eyes and looked at me. "Cherish, God, you feel so good," he groaned. "I don't think I'm going to last very long."

He began to move, slowly at first, and to my surprise, sharp desire began to build inside me again. The heat of him, the exquisite fullness of having him inside me, was something I had been craving when I lay alone in my bed at night, but I had no idea it would be this good. As he moved inside me, my body began to take over again, my hips thrusting up to meet his. We rocked together, finding our own private rhythm, and then Levi started to move harder, to push more deeply inside me. We locked eyes, climbing higher and higher together, and suddenly a second orgasm slammed through me. I cried out, feeling myself pulsate around him, and a few moments later, Levi thrust deeply one final time, then tensed and emptied himself inside me with a loud, powerful groan.

He pulled me toward him as our orgasms began to subside, and then fell onto the bed with me in his arms, still pulsing inside me. He enveloped me in his powerful embrace, our legs entangled. "Cherish," he whispered.

I closed my eyes, feeling such bliss that I had to fight the urge to cry. I didn't trust my voice, so I said nothing, but merely snuggled into his chest. I must have dozed off, because when I came back to the surface Levi's breathing had slowed, and he was softly stroking my hair.

"Levi," I whispered.

"Hey, babe," he murmured, kissing me on the top of the head. "You slept there for a little bit."

"I think I did," I agreed.

"You know, in all the excitement, you never told me how your phone calls went this morning," he said. "Did you learn anything."

"Oh, I can't believe I forgot!" I cried, propping myself up on my elbow to look at him. "I called the Brower County Courthouse in Arizona and had them look up any marriage license information for Isaiah Whitehead and Cherish Holmes. They said that there is no marriage on record for me, but that Isaiah is legally married to Carolyn, his first wife." I smiled up at him. "So I really can call myself Cherish Holmes. I never really was a Whitehead." Knowing that made me feel free somehow, almost as if everything that had happened since I was forced into Isaiah's bed had been a nightmare.

"That's great, babe," he said, brushing back a lock of my hair that had fallen into my face.

"I also asked them to send me an original of my birth certificate," I continued. "I didn't think they would do it, actually, because yesterday at the courthouse here, they said I would need documentation like a driver's license, which of course I don't have yet. But the man I talked to said that he knew my family name and could look up the record, so as long as I filled out and printed the form, I could send it to him personally with a check for the certificate fee. I thought maybe I could ask Seton to write me a check, for now, since I don't have a bank account yet."

I lay back against Levi's chest and curled myself next to him. So much had changed in the past few days. I told myself that I would make sure to print out the form the man on the phone had told me to send to him, and fill it out this weekend so I could send it out right away on Monday. I sighed happily. It really felt like my new life was beginning, and that I was finally safe. Little did I know what I was about to set in motion.

Lying there next to Levi, it almost felt wrong that I could feel so happy when something bad had just happened to the club. But Levi seemed to feel it, too. I had never seen him so relaxed, his hard body seemed completely free of tension as he held me in his arms. For a few minutes, the two of us just lay in bed, content. I wished like anything we could just stay there indefinitely. But I knew that we didn't have much time before Levi would have to go and begin to deal with whatever had just happened.

Sighing, I raised my head to look at him. "Maybe you should tell me what's going on downstairs."

He nodded. "Yeah. So," he murmured as he continued to my hair absently. "Basically, the club has a problem, and we think it's another rival club called the Cannibals. This attack almost has to be them. So we're gonna go into lockdown. That means that no one enters or leaves here but the brothers until we've made sure the problem has been dealt with and there's no more danger to anyone connected with the club."

I snuggled deeper into his chest. "You'll be in danger, out there." It wasn't a question.

Putting a finger under my chin, he raised my face to his. "I've been in danger before. I'll be fine. But I need to know you're safe here." He kissed me deeply.

"Okay." I knew it was all I could do for him. I intended to make sure I wasn't a distraction while he was out there doing whatever it was he needed to do.

We rose from the bed and got dressed silently. It

was time to go help create some order out of the chaos. When we got downstairs, more people had arrived. A few clusters of women and children were gathered in the main room, and still others were carrying boxes of groceries and other supplies into the kitchen.

"Wow," I marveled. "Are these the men's families?"

"Yeah. All the men will bring their old ladies and children here, if they have them." He looked at me and smiled grimly. "On the plus side, this way you get to meet everybody."

Seton spotted us standing at the foot of the stairs, and she broke away from the group she was talking to and came toward us. "Hey," she said, giving me a brief hug. She nodded back toward the shattered glass on the ground. "Crazy, eh?"

"Yeah," Levi muttered. "Crazy. As in, the motherfuckers who did this are crazy to think they won't pay."

Seton smiled sadly at him. "Repo uploaded the surveillance videos to one of the laptops. Grey and the others are in the game room watching it with him now."

Levi looked at me. "I'm gonna go check it out." He leaned down and brushed my lips softly with his, then turned and headed down the long hallway next to the stairs.

Seton raised her eyebrows at me in surprise. "Well, now. What do we have here?"

A flush swept across my cheeks, and I cleared my throat. "Uh… nothing?" I squeaked.

She smirked. "Nothing, my ass. When did you and Mr. Tall, Dark, and Brooding get together?"

"I don't know if we're *together*," I protested. But my stomach dropped at the sudden realization that maybe I was just a quick fling for Levi. I wasn't sure why, but the thought had never occurred to me. Maybe it was because in our community, people didn't have intimate relations with anyone until after they were married. *Maybe this is only something casual for him.* I tried to swallow around the giant lump that had just formed in my throat.

"Well, from the way he looked at you just now, I don't think it's much of a question," she said with a twinkle in her eye.

I shifted my gaze to the east wall, where some of

the men were putting up thick plastic over the broken windows. "I don't know," I confessed softly. "But I do know I like him. He's… different than you'd think. Alone, he's not so hard."

Seton grinned. "I know what you mean. When I met Grey, he was as mean and gruff as they come. Turned out, though, he was more bark than bite, at least with me." Her eyes followed mine to the broken windows. "I think whoever's responsible for this is about to feel his bite, though."

I hugged my arms around myself, suddenly feeling cold. "I don't like to think about some of the things those men do."

"That's why they don't tell us much. It's part of protecting us. The club's like a family, and that extends to the women and children. Once you're part of it, any one of them will go to the ends of the earth to keep you safe."

"How long are we going to be locked in here?" I asked her.

"Not long, I'd guess. Depends on how long it takes the men to figure out who's behind this, but Grey said he has a pretty good idea. Once they know…" her voice trailed off, leaving me to imagine what the fate of those responsible would be.

After a few moments of silence, Seton handed me a broom. "Come on. Come help me clean up some of this glass. And I'll introduce you to some of the other women."

Over the next few hours, I swept, cleaned, cooked, and worried with the other women. Seton introduced me to Jules, who was Repo's old lady, and a bunch of others who ranged in age from their early twenties to my mother's age. When Seton told them I was with Levi, I got a few good-natured winks and more than a few indiscreet questions about his performance in bed, but I could tell it was all in fun. Even more, they seemed to instantly accept me as one of their own.

That evening, as I looked around at the women getting their children ready for bed and the men standing guard by the door, I felt more like I was part of a family than I ever had. It was funny, even after spending my entire life in a community that was all about protecting itself from the outside world, I had to leave for the outside to find a place where I felt truly accepted for who I was, no questions asked.

CHAPTER 14

Levi

The men and I sat silently sprawled on the long leather couch in the game room as Repo brought up the footage from the surveillance cam on the big projection screen. Usually when I came in here, it was to blow off some steam by kicking someone else's ass at Call of Duty or GTA. Instead, we were watching video of the men who had set off a fucking pipe bomb at our clubhouse. Those pieces of shit were about to find themselves starring in their own real-life version of a first-person shooter.

"That one, on the right," Trig said. "I know him.

His name's Nacho, or Enchilada, or some shit." He shook his head in disgust. "These stupid fuckers didn't even have the sense to disguise themselves."

The quality of the video was good, and showed three men well enough to be able to identify them by their features. Two of them I could clearly recognize as members of the Cannibals, and Moose said he recognized the third.

"Oh, this is good. This is very good," Winger said with a sadistic grin. He was going to enjoy what came next. We all were.

"This is all I need to know." Grey's voice had gone cold and hard as steel. "These fuckers are gonna pay for this. And one of them is going to pay dearly for Hammer's death. With his life."

With this footage in our possession, it was clear to us all who had been behind all of the recent anonymous attacks on the Stone Kings. First, the ambush that had killed Grey's best friend Hammer. Then, the drive-by at Maisie's diner. And now, this. It was time to mete out some serious club justice. The only question now was how, and when.

"I want to know which one of those sons of bitches shot the bullet that killed Hammer," Grey spat out. "That one's mine." The look of pure rage on his face would have made anyone on the receiving end's blood run cold. There would be no question that Grey would avenge Hammer's death. I almost felt sorry for the poor fucker who would end his days staring up at the face of someone who would show him absolutely no mercy.

"We know where the Cannibals' clubhouse is, up in Cooperton." I sat up and addressed them all. "I think we're gonna need to pick these guys up. They're gonna take a little ride with us. I bet they can be persuaded to give up the name of who killed him."

"These guys are gonna feel some pain," Moose agreed. But what about Skull?" Moose asked. "This all started after he took over as president of the Cannibals."

I nodded. "We need to take care of him, as well."

Grey had just opened his mouth to reply when Frankenstein appeared in the doorway.

"Hey, boss. Found this outside."

He lumbered into the room and handed Grey a small piece of cloth, then flung his hulking frame down in an empty leather armchair. Grey's eyes went even more black with fury as he turned the cloth over in his hand.

"Son of a bitch," he bit out.

"What is it?" Trig asked.

Grey held it up for us to see. It was a patch with a few long, stray threads hanging from it, apparently ripped from an MC cut. Only one word was sewn on it:

Aztecs.

"What the fuck?" Repo exploded. "What in the goddamn *fuck*? Lalo was lying to us!"

"Jesus Christ!" murmured Cal.

"The fucking *cartel* pipe bombed us? This is war!" yelled Moose.

The men began shouting over one another, swearing blood and vengeance no matter the cost. As I sat there listening to them, my brain turned this new information over in my head. Something wasn't right.

"I don't buy it," I finally said, cutting into their argument.

"Don't buy what?" Grey asked, turning to me.

"It's too easy. What, are we supposed to believe that this patch just happened to rip off a cut while they were getting ready to throw the bomb?"

"Maybe they left it on purpose. Like a calling card."

"That doesn't make any sense." I ran my hand through my hair. "Look. All the other attacks were anonymous. Now, not long after we talk to Lalo, suddenly this one can be easily traced back to the Aztecs? Nah. They're fuckin' with us. Trying to lead us in the direction they want us to go. They're hoping we're too angry and too out for blood to think straight."

I looked at Grey. "I think Skull is trying to play us. He's trying to get us to go after the Aztecs, to consider Lalo our enemy. He's trying to get us to break the conditions of the truce by striking back at them."

"Why the fuck would he do that?" Trig challenged, but I could tell he was considering my words.

"I dunno," I shrugged. "Maybe he's after control of the cartel. If Skull can make it so Lalo looks to his men like he can't control things, Lalo comes out looking like a weak leader to the other people in the cartel. If Skull can make a play to take him down, he could slip into the power vacuum, then set himself up as the ringleader. Shit," I added. "Maybe he's even hoping we'll take Lalo out for him."

"That's fucked up," Cal muttered.

"Maybe," I admitted. "But we don't know Skull at all, besides the one meet we had with him where we knew right away he was lying through his teeth. All we know is, at least two of the men who just bombed us are Cannibals, probably all three if Moose is right. And we know Lalo brought Skull to the meet with us, which means Skull seems to be worming his way in to a position of trust. It strikes me as a lot more likely that the Aztecs patch was planted without Lalo's knowledge, than that there was an Aztec involved with the bombing but the camera just happened not to pick him up."

"Yeah," Grey nodded, considering. "Yeah. And another thing: this bomb wasn't big enough to kill any of us, not unless one of us had been standing right near it when it went off. It was just enough to cause some damage, stir the hornet's nest. What Levi is saying makes sense."

"So, what are we gonna do?" Repo asked.

"We're gonna grab these guys," Grey replied, pointing a finger at the screen. "We take them in their territory, then bring them back here and interrogate them. One of them is gonna give up the guy who shot Hammer, or else he's gonna die in his place. Then we take what we know to Lalo. Tell him he's got a choice: either he takes care of Skull, or we will. His reaction should tell us a lot about whether the cartel is behind this."

"Agreed," Trig said.

"Yup," Repo added.

I nodded.

We hashed out a few of the details for grabbing the men in the video. Seven of the men would go into Cannibals territory, taking a cage and a van between them, and a big enough cache of weapons to last them through any unforeseen circumstances. They'd bring the men back to our turf, to the barn of an abandoned farmstead we sometimes used.

We'd interrogate them until they talked. It wasn't likely to be pretty. We would do whatever was necessary to get them to admit the Cannibals were responsible for all the recent attacks on our club, and tell us what the fuck Skull was up to. And we'd make it clear they needed to give up the name of the man responsible for killing Hammer. If they didn't talk, Grey would choose one of them, and end him instead.

I was betting they would talk.

Back out in the main room of the clubhouse, things were mostly cleaned up from the explosion, except for a thin layer of dust on the floor of the area closest to where the blast had occurred. The windows would have to be replaced as soon as it was feasible, and Grey told Winger to get in touch with one of the local outfits we occasionally did business with the next day.

The women had made sure that all the kids had gotten fed, and upstairs I could hear the sounds of young people running around and arguing with their moms about bedtime. The younger ones didn't have any concept that they were here because of any danger; they were just caught up in the excitement of camping out at the clubhouse. To them, it was just a giant slumber party.

Trig came up behind me and cocked his head, grinning. "Buncha hellions up there, ain't they?"

"No shit."

"Some a' those kids would give you more of a run for your money than a fuckin' Cannibal," he chuckled.

I listened to the rhythmic pounding of their feet as they ran around, shrieking and yelling to each other. Kids were never something that had really been on my radar. Most of the ones I encountered out and about in Lupine were scared shitless of me. These kids, growing up around the MC like they had, knew that tattoos and leather didn't mean shit when it came to children. I mostly gave them a wide berth, but I had to admit a few of them were pretty cute. The big, tough badasses of the club who were their daddies or their "uncles" became putty in the hands of these kids. Like Repo said to me once, it didn't matter how rough and tough you were; when a two year-old hands you a toy phone, you answer it.

I cast a glance across the room, where Cherish was helping Winger's old lady Monica corral their two twin boys into some pajamas. I found myself wondering whether Cherish wanted kids someday. I remembered what she said about the final straw that made her decide to leave the WFZ Ranch: she didn't want her daughters to grow up without any choices of their own. She would be a good mom, I was sure of it. She would teach her sons to be good, decent men, and teach her daughters to stand up for themselves. Something swelled in my chest as I imagined a bright, cherubic little girl, with auburn hair that streamed behind her as she ran, and Cherish's penetrating brown eyes.

As though she could feel my eyes on her, Cherish looked up then, noticed me watching her, and flashed me a wide, radiant smile. Trigger caught the look she gave me, and nodded her direction. "That Cherish sure is somethin'," he said casually.

I cut my eyes toward him. "Yeah?" I asked, my voice suddenly sharp. "Whaddya mean by that?"

His face broke into a shit-eating grin. "Oh, nothin'," he said. "Just makin' an observation." He was silent a moment. "A man could do a lot worse than havin' her in his bed."

"I thought I told you Cherish was strictly off limits," I warned.

He chuckled. "Yeah, but I thought that was because you were tryin' to protect her, not that you wanted to get there first." I opened my mouth to respond, but he cut me off. "Don't tell me I'm wrong. I see the way you look at her. You're a lucky fucker, if she'll have you. Don't mess it up, brother."

"I am not having this conversation with you," I retorted.

"Suit yourself. I never said a goddamn word." He was silent for a moment, then took a long pull of his beer. "Hey, is it true you were raised in some fundie cult?"

"Fuck off, Trig," I said, shoving him. He laughed and wandered away to go piss off someone else.

We were technically still in lockdown, but I needed some air to clear my head, so I went out back and told the brother guarding the door that I was gonna go make a sweep of the perimeter. As I walked out into the dark night, gazing at the stars, I thought more about Cherish. My feelings about her were a complete fucking mess. I had tried as hard as I could to stay away from her, but it was hopeless. There was just something about her that made me into a fucking moony teenager around her. She was so innocently sexy, like she had no idea that men stopped whatever they were doing and stared after her whenever she walked by. She was so completely inexperienced sexually, and yet the woman who was awakening in her under my touch was sensual, sexy, and wanton. The sounds of her cries of pleasure as I licked her to orgasm echoed in my head, making my dick harden instantly in my pants.

I shook out a smoke and lit it, and tried to focus on something else, but it was no use. I wanted her again, right now. I knew I wouldn't be able to stay away from her, now that I knew what it was like to be inside her. I had fucked a lot of women in my time, but I had never seemed to be able to conjure up much interest in any of them once the initial mystery of what they were like in bed was solved. I had watched other brothers meet someone and fall in love, and each time I would shake my head inwardly, wondering how they could face the idea of spending the rest of their lives with one woman. Now here I was, looking at Cherish and trying to picture what our kid would look like if we had one.

Shit.

It wasn't fair to her, I told myself. She'd only just recently emerged from the artificial world of the WFZ Ranch. She barely knew what real life was even like yet. And I was the first man outside the ranch she had even had a conversation of more than a couple of sentences with. And even though she had been married, I knew I was the first man to ever make her come. I could tell I was by the shocked look on her face that first night when she rode my hand to orgasm. She had had no idea what was about to happen until I pushed her over the edge. My already-throbbing dick strained against my zipper. God *damn*. I wanted to do that again. I wanted to make her scream with pleasure, in every possible position, in every damn way I knew how. I could probably spend the rest of my life devoted to the sole mission of making Cherish Holmes come.

I wanted her bad, worse than I had ever wanted a woman in my life. Hell, maybe I was even a little in love with her. She was more than I could ever have hoped for in a woman. She was fucking gorgeous, smart, independent... Shit, I wasn't just crazy about her, I *admired* her. She had left everything she'd ever known and struck out on her own, with hardly a cent to her name and only the name of some stranger who might just as well turn her away as help her. As tough as it had been for me to leave the Ranch, it would have been a hundred times harder for her. And whereas I had created a shell of armor with my tattoos to keep the past away, Cherish approached the world with a brave vulnerability I couldn't help but respect.

Cherish was something special. Any man with a brain in his head could see that. But she had barely had time to get used to the idea that she was no longer Cherish Whitehead, but Cherish Holmes, a woman whose life had yet to be written. How could I even think of asking her to stay with me — to try to make a future with me — when she hadn't even had a *present* yet?

I swore softly and stared blindly into the night. I should never have let myself give in to my desire to make Cherish's body mine. And now it was too late to change what had happened, even if I wanted to. In a way, I wished I could go back in time, to stop this thing between us before it had started. But the thing was, even though it had probably been a mistake, I couldn't make myself feel sorry about it. I knew I should end it right now, before it went any further. But I couldn't do it. I was too fucking weak. I knew damn well that no matter what I told myself, no matter what promises I made to leave her alone, I wouldn't be able to stay away from her. I knew, just as much as I knew anything, that tonight I would go upstairs to that apartment and make love to her again and again until both of us passed out. Then tomorrow, I'd wake up with her in my arms and do the same damn thing. For as long as she would have me.

But what I could do, for Cherish, was to not ask her for any more than that. It fucking put a knife in my gut to think about her leaving, but it was just a fact that in all likelihood, eventually that was just what would happen. I made a promise to myself that as soon as she was ready, I would let her walk away.

I took a draw on my smoke and let out a short, bitter laugh at the irony of it all: the only woman I had ever known who made me believe in a future was the one woman I couldn't have one with.

CHAPTER 15

Cherish

The lockdown was over by the afternoon of the following day. I never did find out what was going on, but Jules told me that was normal. Club business was kept away from the women and families as much as humanly possible. She said that it had been a long time since the Stone Kings had felt the need to do a lockdown — years, in fact — and that most of the time it was just a precaution. The fact that this time there had been a bomb was shocking to me, but she said that the club never would have kept us in that location if they had thought the clubhouse wasn't secure.

After the excitement had died down and things started going back to normal, I found myself spending more time with Seton and Jules, and some of the other "old ladies" I had met during the lockdown. I even spent a few afternoons babysitting for some of their kids. It was fun to be around children again. I hadn't realized how much I had missed my own stepchildren until I was listening to pre-teen girls chattering excitedly about a song they liked or some movie they wanted to see. Their freedom and happiness made a strong impression on me, and I couldn't help but feel a pang of sadness that my oldest stepdaughter would soon be married, her childhood essentially over.

My own life started taking on a more "normal" routine, as well. Levi showed up at the clubhouse one day with a school ID for me, with my picture on it saying I was a graduate of Coyote Falls High School. Armed with the school identification card, I was finally able to go take my driving test at the Colorado DMV. Seton told me I could use her mailing address for the test, and that I could go change it once I was living someplace permanent.

She drove me there and vouched for me, bringing her own license as proof of her address and saying I was living with her. I held my breath until the dour woman behind the counter finally said she would accept Seton's ID as proof of my address.

I had been super nervous about the tests themselves, but I passed both the written test and the driving test on the first try. I was beaming as I stood for my license photograph, and even though I looked incredibly silly when the photographer showed me the image, I didn't ask for him to take another one. It would be a reminder for me whenever I looked at it of how far I had come to get it.

About two weeks after I sent off my application for a birth certificate, it came for me in the mail, which meant that I could finally officially start my job as a hostess at Hammie's Bar and Restaurant. The first few days at Hammie's were intimidating, even though everyone I had met there went out of their way to be nice to me. Having never had a job before, I kept worrying about messing up, but people were so understanding, and the manager, Angela, made sure that all my shifts were during slow times at first, until I got used to the pace of the job.

One of the best things that happened during that period was something that anyone else would have passed off as completely unimportant, but to me it was everything. I had just finished a shift at Hammie's and was walking to the bank to open an account with my very first paycheck. On my way there, a car slowed down and a woman with a small boy in the passenger seat stuck her head out. "Excuse me, can you tell me where Primrose Elementary School is?" she asked. "We just moved into town."

"Sure," I smiled, pointing down the road. "You just follow this street about four more blocks, and take a left on Primrose Street. Then from there it's about three more blocks."

"Thank you!" the child yelled, flashing me a gap-toothed grin.

I watched them drive away, feeling a burst of pride and gratitude I would have had a hard time explaining to anyone else but Levi. The woman and her son had mistaken me for a native of Lupine, I realized. But more importantly, she had mistaken me for someone *normal*, someone who fit in to this world that not two months ago had been completely foreign to me. She thought I *belonged* here.

And maybe, I told myself with a surge of hope, just maybe she was right.

Opening my bank account was easier than I had expected, and within an hour, everything was set up, and I had checkbook of my very own, and a shiny new debit card so I could access my money whenever I wanted. *My very own money*, I though with a surge of pride. As I walked down the bank steps with copies of all my paperwork, I made a mental note to tell Levi about everything that had happened today, especially the woman asking me for directions. I blushed a little at the idea of sharing something so silly, but in my heart I knew he'd be happy for me. Levi knew what it was like to feel like an outsider. And I was sure that as much as he tried to push away memories of his past, he hadn't pushed them so far away that he wouldn't remember wanting to belong to something.

With a jolt, I realized that the Stone Kings had probably been that "something" — the thing he had chosen to belong to. A surge of affection coursed through me: in some ways, we were so similar, Levi and I, despite our many obvious differences. He would instinctively understand things about me no one else ever would. Even though at first he had been harsh and distant with me, now he was tender.

Some nights in the dark, after we had finished making love, he would softly begin talking about memories from his childhood, and I understood instinctively that these were not stories he had ever shared with anyone else.

My mood was contemplative as I walked the two blocks back to the restaurant, where the bike that Seton had lent me was parked. I tried not to think too much about the meaning of whatever was happening between Levi and me. In my old world, what we were doing was completely unthinkable, and the echo of the old Cherish would sometimes whisper in my ear that premarital sex was of the Devil. But then I thought about how my so-called marriage to Isaiah had been, and that he and I had never really been legally married anyway. It seemed like by comparison, the relationship that had been "wrong" was that one, not my relationship with Levi now. Levi had awakened something so beautiful and unknown inside me, it was almost as though in a way he had given my body back to me. Under his skillful hands, my skin had learned what it really meant to be touched. With him, I felt like a woman, not a little girl whose only job was to accept a man's needs without complaining, and without ever expecting anything in return.

But what I felt for Levi was more than just physical. I hardly dared to let myself think about it, but he had become someone so important in my life that it felt like my heart was being ripped out of my chest whenever I imagined that someday he might not be there anymore. Sometimes, I forced myself to think about it anyway, as much as it hurt. I told myself that I would have to get used to a life without him eventually. It stood to reason. After all, he was a member of a motorcycle club. As kind as he had been to take me in and let me stay for a while, he didn't need someone like me hanging around. I knew he didn't like to be tied down, and as tender as he was with me, I knew I was a reminder of something he had done everything to forget. Even if this wasn't just some casual thing to him, that was a long way from saying that he would ever want anything permanent with me.

I biked the three miles toward the MC clubhouse, my throat constricting as tears threatened to well up inside and break through. *No,* I told myself fiercely. *Don't cry. You always knew this thing with Levi couldn't last. You're not allowed to cry when you brought it on yourself.* I was fighting to think of something else when I noticed that one of the cars driving in my lane on the highway was not passing me, but instead had slowed down behind me. I glanced over my shoulder to see a dark blue pickup with no front plate, matching my speed about a car length behind my rear tire. Nervously, I pulled over onto the shoulder so that the truck would pass me. As soon as I planted my feet on the gravel and looked back, the pickup gunned its engine and roared past, the passenger window rolling up just in time for me not to see the occupant.

Shaken, I watched the pickup disappear into the distance, then got on my bike and rode the rest of the way to the clubhouse. I made a mental note to tell Seton or Jules about it, and ask them whether they had ever had something like that happen to them.

Back at the clubhouse, I was greeted by Cal, who was just walking out the door as I locked up my bike. "Hey, Cherish, how's it going?" he asked, his now-familiar roguish grin making me smile in spite of myself.

"Good! Look, I have a bank account now!" I pulled my debit card out of my pocket and showed it to him.

"Damn," he whistled. "You're moving up in the world. Don't forget to tell people you knew me when you're famous."

I blushed, but had to laugh. "You're making fun of me!"

"Nah, not really. Seriously, Cherish, that's great. What are you gonna buy with all that cold, hard cash?"

"First on my list is to pay back Seton everything I owe her," I said firmly. "After that, we'll see."

"Well," he winked. "Don't forget to buy something for yourself. This is a big deal, your first paycheck. You should celebrate a little."

I smiled. "Is Levi around?" I asked. Suddenly I couldn't wait to tell him about my day. He'd probably tease me about the bank account, too, but I knew he would be proud of me.

"He'll probably be back in a little while. He's gone on a run with Grey and a few of the others."

I tried to mask my disappointment. "Oh, okay, thanks."

Since I couldn't share my good news with Levi, I called Seton instead and probably talked her ear off about my day. Like a true friend, she was almost happier than I was about everything. In all my excitement, it completely slipped my mind until later to ask her about the strange blue pickup, and by the time I remembered it that night, the whole incident didn't seem that important anymore. *Probably just some random men who felt like being jerks*, I told myself, and forgot about it.

That night, around ten o'clock, Levi showed up at my door. I had been planning to tell him about my day straight off, but as soon as his eyes met mine my body seemed to turn to liquid. Wordlessly, he leaned down and picked me up in his strong arms, kicking the door shut behind him. His lips came down on mine hungrily as he closed the distance to the bedroom in just a few steps. All thoughts of the day vanished as he knelt on the bed and set me down. As it always had been between us, this time felt like the very first: my body felt electric with excitement, desperate for his touch. The only difference now was that I craved it with even more intensity because I knew what he could do to me.

Levi pulled his shirt off over his head impatiently and lifted mine up, exposing the black lace bra that I had put on this morning for the first time. "Jesus," he groaned as his eyes grew wide. "Cherish, you're gonna kill me one of these days."

Bravely, I reached down to cup the hard steel

straining under the fly of his jeans. He gasped at my touch. "I don't want to kill you, Levi," I breathed. "I just want you to want me."

He laughed deep and low in his throat. "Mission accomplished. You could be wearing a wooden barrel and you'd still be the sexiest fucking thing I've ever seen."

I giggled as I remembered the bra I'd arrived in, which Seton had forced me to get rid of. Levi might be telling the truth, but I sure was glad I didn't have to test it.

"What are you giggling about, little girl?" he demanded in a fake-angry voice. "I'll give you something to laugh about." He growled loudly as his head dipped toward my breasts, and I shrieked, then clapped my hand over my mouth and began laughing even harder. My giggles turned quickly to moans of pleasure as his mouth found my nipples through the cloth and bit them softly, teasing the nipples into hardness as I writhed under his touch. My arms went around his head, my hands fisting in his hair as he continued his sweet torment. Warmth flooded through me, and I felt myself getting wet as my core began to throb.

"Levi," I breathed. "Oh, God, Levi… yes." I

ached for him to take me, to pull my clothes off and enter me. I needed him inside me, needed to feel myself pulsing around his hard length. But first, I wanted something else. As he pulled away from my breasts and began to push me back down on the bed, I stopped him. "Wait. Not yet." I slid off the bed and finished removing my tank, throwing it to the floor, then knelt by the side of the bed. With trembling hands, I reached for the waistband of his jeans and pulled until he was standing next to the bed facing me.

Slowly, I undid the button, then the zipper, then tugged downward until his jeans were in a pool on the floor. His thick, hard length stood at attention, rising and falling as it pulsed in front of me. "Cherish," Levi began, but I stopped him. "Shhh. I've been wanting to do this for so long," I breathed.

Before Levi, I had never touched a man intimately. Now, my mouth watered and I parted my lips, hoping I wouldn't make a fool of myself. I gazed in awe at how beautiful he was, then leaned forward and lapped at the head with the flat of my tongue, like I would an ice cream cone. Levi froze, and drew in his breath sharply. I licked him again, swirling my tongue around him, marveling at how soft and hot the skin was, and how hard it was underneath. Opening my lips further, I closed them around the head, and sucked softly as my tongue licked and swirled.

He fisted a hand in my hair and swore softly. "Fuck, Cherish. That's… Oh, fuck…"

I pulled back, unsure. "What?" I asked, gazing up at him. "Is it not good?"

His laughter was so sudden that it startled me. "Cherish, that may be the best fucking thing I've ever felt in my life," he rumbled.

"So I should keep going?" I asked, a smile tugging at my lips.

"Yes, you should keep going," he grinned down at me sexily. "But I'm gonna stop you before it's too late. I need to be inside you tonight."

Before it's too late… He meant before he came, I knew. The thought of me giving him an orgasm like that made me feel almost dizzy with excitement. I wanted to do that for him, I realized. I wanted to feel him in my mouth as he got closer and closer. I wanted to taste him, to know him, to be the one to give him so much pleasure that he lost control. I knew he wouldn't let me do it tonight, but I told myself that I would do it soon. My lips closed softly over him again and I began to suck and swirl, bobbing my head slowly down his shaft, taking him deeper into my mouth with every thrust. Levi groaned loudly, and the sound went straight to my throbbing center. I could taste him, salty and hot, and I began to bob more quickly, needing more.

Levi swore loudly and pulled my head away. "You make it damn hard to keep my resolve, babe," he said through gritted teeth. "But I have other plans."

He grabbed my arms and pulled me up, then threw me on the bed unceremoniously. I shrieked again and began to laugh, then my laughter turned to moans as he made quick work of my shorts and panties. He spread my legs and plunged his tongue deep inside me. "You taste so fucking good, Cherish," he growled. "Do you know I fantasize about tasting you when you're not with me? I think about licking you, fucking you with my tongue, and it's all I can do to not drop everything I'm doing and come bury my face between your legs."

I cried out as my hips rose to meet his mouth. "Levi!"

"Yes, say my name," he murmured against my

skin. "Say my fucking name. Say you're mine. All mine."

"I'm yours," I panted.

"Damn right you're mine." He drew his tongue lazily over my swollen lips, and I cried out again. "You belong to me. *This* belongs to me." Sucking me between his lips, he began to press and flick gently at my nub, pulling back just enough as I strained toward him to drive me wild with need. My legs spread wide, my thighs tensed, as I began to plead with him, my hands desperately trying to pull his head closer.

"Please, Levi!" I cried in a strangled voice. "Please let me come!"

A groan emerged from deep in his throat, and with one final lick he pushed me over the edge. I called out his name as the waves crashed over me, his tongue pulling every last spasm from me until I couldn't take anymore and pushed his head gently away. I felt him get off the bed, then come back. Then he was leaning over me, pulling my waist toward his kneeling form.

"Do you know what you do to me when you beg me?" he demanded. His eyes were locked on mine as he opened the condom wrapper, then rolled the condom over his erection. Positioning himself between my legs, he pushed his pulsing member against my entrance. My eyes closed, my head arched back as he entered me. He lifted my legs up, placing my ankles over his shoulders, and thrust into me, over and over, deeper each time. A loud moan ripped from my throat as I felt my desire return. I opened my eyes to find his locked on me. One large, muscled hand held me by the waist. The second reached forward and his thumb slid against my slick nub, making me gasp. "Levi!" My whisper turned into a moan.

"I'm close, Cherish," he rumbled. "So close. Come with me, baby." His thrusts continued, harder and deeper, the swipes of his thumb timed with them, and suddenly, my thighs tensed and I screamed, coming even harder this time, so hard it felt like I was flying apart. A few seconds later, Levi groaned my name and froze, then emptied himself inside me, every pulse of his orgasm echoing the throbbing of my own.

Levi pulled me up so I was sitting on his lap. He was still inside me, and I wished we could stay like that forever. He felt so right filling me up, my legs wrapped around him. I wanted time to stop, for us to be able to just lie there, making love forever, joined as though we were one.

Eventually, he pulled out of me, and went to the bathroom to dispose of the condom. He came back, turned off the lights, and got into bed beside me. I snuggled into the crook of his arm and told him about my day. Levi listened while I prattled on about my new bank account and how proud I was that someone had mistaken me for a local, but he seemed preoccupied, though he tried to hide it. I hadn't noticed anything unusual about his mood when he came through the door, but I reasoned that even if there had been something, I probably wouldn't have noticed. After all, it wasn't like we'd spent much time chatting before he picked me up and brought me to bed.

I was a little disappointed that he didn't seem happier for me, but told myself that I was being silly. I chalked his distractedness up to club business and didn't push it, knowing that if it was club business, he likely wouldn't tell me anything about it anyway.

Eventually, I stopped talking, and he held me in his arms and kissed me until we fell asleep some time later. In the morning, when I woke up, he was already gone.

CHAPTER 16

Levi

I had slipped out of Cherish's bed just as it was beginning to get light. It was harder than hell leaving her like that, all warm and soft and beautiful, but I needed some time to clear my head. The club had some serious business to attend to in the days ahead, and I needed to be focused for it.

But most of all, I needed to be away from Cherish's gorgeous body so that I could think.

Last night had been a mistake, I knew. A serious

one. Oh, I had gone to her bed like I knew I would, had licked her and fucked her until she was screaming my name. It was maybe the best night of my life, and at the time I had felt happier than I could ever remember feeling, as I turned off the light and felt Cherish sink into my arms like she was born to be there.

All that wouldn't have been so bad, except I couldn't keep my damn mouth shut. In my passion, I needed to hear her call my name, to tell me she was mine, all mine. I ordered her to say it, over and over, and she had, with no hesitation.

I had had no right to do that to her. I had promised myself that even though I was falling for her, I wouldn't try to hold her back. I had sworn to myself that I would let her walk away as soon as she got her feet under her. Now, here she was, finally earning some money, getting her license... hell, pretty soon I figured she'd be renting an apartment somewhere in Lupine. She'd be moving out of the clubhouse any week now. But instead of keeping my emotions in check, in the heat of passion I'd said to her exactly what I had been trying to hide, even from myself: I wanted her. I wanted her to be mine. The thought of another man touching her, doing the things to her I had... it made me want to murder people. But I had no right to tell her any of that. If I couldn't keep it light between us, I shouldn't be with her at all. *I should be pulling away from her, giving her space, not claiming her body and soul.* And I realized, I couldn't keep it light anymore.

But I wasn't sure I could pull away, either.

Days went by. The club talked out our strategy, and scouts went undercover into Cannibals territory to do some recon and get a bead on the comings and goings of the men we'd identified from the surveillance tape. I buried myself in club business, and tried to ignore Cherish, hoping that after a few days she'd get sick of my indifference and forget about me. The idea was like a knife in my chest, but I couldn't figure out any other way to do it. Whenever she was anywhere near me, the pull toward her was so strong I couldn't fight against it. So the only option I had was to make sure that I interacted with her as little as possible.

One morning about a week later, I woke as the sun was rising, took a hot shower, and brewed a pot of coffee. As with every morning, my dreams had been about Cherish, and I woke with her name on my lips. By the time I was finishing my second cup, I was so damn disgusted with myself for mooning over her that I finally pushed her out of my mind and forced myself to focus on the day ahead. In a few hours, Moose, Repo, Sag and the boys would be back with the three Cannibals they had nabbed outside a biker bar in Cooperton the night before. Moose had phoned Grey to let them know that they had picked up all three of the men from the video, plus one prospect who had the misfortune to have been with them. I smiled grimly when Grey called to tell me the news. That prospect was gonna get one hell of a trial by fire.

The men would be at the abandoned farm with their captives by around six this morning. Grey planned to give them a few hours to stew in their own juices before the rest of us showed up. Around ten, I rode over to the clubhouse and met the other brothers, and we headed out to the farmstead. When we got there, we parked our bikes behind the large barn we used for interrogations and deals. Inside, Winger, Repo and the others were standing around smoking. Four men were tied up on rickety chairs in the center of the space.

"Smells like Cannibal in here," Trig called loudly, referring to the slight aroma of manure that still hung in the air from the barn's working days.

"Fuck you," spat one of the men, a wiry, hook-nosed man with long, greasy hair.

"Ooohhh, you're mighty spunky for someone who's tied up like a little farm animal," Repo said easily, sidling up to the man's chair. "You wanna repeat that into the mic?" he asked, holding his fist close to the man. "No? I didn't think so."

"Man, what do you want with us?" the prospect yelled, trying to put on a brave face.

"You, little man, should probably shut the fuck up," I retorted, glancing over at him. "You stay out of the way, then you'll only have to watch this. You keep flappin' your gums, you're likely to get hurt." The prospect fell silent.

"Though," I continued, turning to the others. "He does ask a pertinent question. Why are you here? What do we want with you? Any of you wanna know the answer to that?"

"I'm pretty sure they know already," Grey said quietly. "I'm pretty sure they know exactly why the fuck they're here."

"I got no fuckin' idea, *ese*," sneered a stocky man with shaggy hair and a prison pussy. "I think you got the wrong men. We were just having a few beers, minding our own business, when your boys picked us up."

"I'm glad you were enjoying yourselves," countered Grey. "Because those might be the last beers you ever drink." In the corner, the prospect moaned quietly, but said nothing.

"Yo, what's this all about, man? Cuz I seriously have no idea." This one was muscled and square-jawed, and seemed to think he actually had a chance of convincing us they were innocent.

"Fuck this," Trig muttered. He leaned down and punched Square Jaw hard in the gut. Air rushed out of his lungs at the blow, and he coughed and gasped for breath, looking up at Trig with unconcealed loathing.

"You pieces of shit have fucked with the Stone Kings for the last time," Grey said. "We know you were behind the attack that killed one of our men a few months ago. We know you shot out Maisie's Diner. And we know you bombed our fuckin' clubhouse."

"Whoa, whoa, whoa," Square Jaw wheezed, shaking his head. "Man, we ain't done none of that.

You got it all wrong, man."

"Not interested in hearing your bullshit," I barked.

"You ain't got no proof, *ese*," the stocky one with the prison pussy scoffed. "You don't know it was us, you just guessing."

"Surveillance cameras, fuckface," Winger retorted with a smirk, holding up a thumb drive. He stepped forward and punched Prison Pussy in the face. A loud crack echoed throughout the barn as his nose broke. With a low gurgle, the man's head lolled to one side, blood mixing with spittle drooling from his mouth. He wasn't out, but about as close to it as you could come. Winger's punches were insanely accurate, which was good. We needed them all conscious. For now.

The prospect was getting pretty worked up now, squirming in his chair and I could hear his breathing coming hard and fast from fear. "You want to shut up," I said harshly, pointing my finger at him. "Best thing you can do for yourself is to make us forget you're even here." He went instantly silent and still, and I almost laughed wondering if he would pass out from trying not to even breathe.

"So," Grey cut in, nodding at Prison Pussy. "Now that we've got your attention. Talk."

"We don't know —" Hook Nose began.

The heel of my boot connected with his jaw with a sickening crunch. "You are about to lose your ability to say a fucking thing, so choose your words wisely," I bit out. "We. Know. What. You. Did. We know the Cannibals are responsible for these attacks." I turned to Square Jaw and sent stiff fingertips right into his windpipe, pinching just short of crushing it. "You. Talk."

His eyes were streaming tears of pain. "What do you want to know?" he choked out.

I eased the pressure on his windpipe just a little. "You're gonna tell us which one of you was responsible for killing our man Hammer. For starters."

"I don't know, man," he blurted out. "There was a few of us there that night. He got in front of a bullet. I don't know whose it was."

"You'd better figure it out, soon," Grey said, his voice low and threatening. "Because the Cannibals are gonna pay for Hammer's death with a life. If you gentlemen don't know who it is, it's gonna have to be at least one of you."

"At least," I agreed.

"I swear, we don't know!" Square Jaw's eyes were wild.

"Let's move on for a moment," Grey continued. "Recognize this?" He held up the Aztecs patch. None of the three men responded.

Trig drew back and backhanded Prison Pussy, hard. "The man asked you a question," he rasped, pulling the man's head up by the hair and forcing him to focus on Grey.

He gurgled and spat blood, then said, "Skull told us to leave it there."

"Why?" Grey barked, taking a step forward. Trig pulled harder on the man's hair to make him respond.

"I don't know!" he said. "He wanted to throw you off the track!"

"He wanted us to think it was the Aztecs?" Grey's voice was hard. "And risk a full-out war with the cartel?"

"We don't know why, man," Prison Pussy said. "He said he was operating under Aztec orders."

Trig looked at me and raised his eyebrows. No one spoke for a moment.

"Let's go back to our brother Hammer's death," Repo spoke up. "I'm sure you fellas have had a few moments to search your memories. You happen to have any recollection of who's responsible?"

For a moment, none of them moved or spoke. Grey sighed. "Okay, then," and drew his gun from the waistband of his pants. "I guess you all get to go together!"

"NO!" shouted Prison Pussy suddenly. His wide, wild eyes went to Hook Nose, then shifted quickly to Square Jaw. Something unspoken passed between them. Then Square Jaw opened his mouth and blurted, "It's him, man. Flaco did it."

Hook Nose's face contorted in fury. He let loose a string of words in Spanish, his body flailing in the chair as though he itched to get loose and kill his comrades.

Trig broke into a wide grin. "I think we've found our man, brothers."

Grey nodded once, which sent Hook Nose into another tirade. Trig pulled out his gun and backhanded him with it. "That's enough now," he said easily. "No reason to use off-color language."

I addressed the other three men, including the prospect. "Looks like you lucky fuckers get to live today. But unfortunately, you're gonna have to watch your friend here die. When we dump you back in your territory, make sure you give the message to Skull that we've taken back what was ours."

I turned on my heel and walked out of the barn for a smoke. A few others followed, leaving Grey to do what he needed to do. As I sat on a low rock and enjoyed my cigarette, an occasional scream drifted toward me from the barn. Eventually, a single gunshot rang out. Trig emerged a minute or so later.

"Well, that's done," he said simply. "Poor prospect lost his lunch when Grey shot that motherfucker. I ain't sure he's gonna make it as a Cannibal."

I chuckled grimly. "What about the other two?"

"The fucker with the goat beard is acting all macho again, now that he knows he ain't gettin' killed. I had to backhand him with my gun to get him to shut up." He smiled. "Felt good."

"We about done here?" I asked him. I stubbed out the butt of my cigarette and stood.

"Yeah. Winger, Repo, and the men'll dispose of the body and take the others back tonight," he continued.

Just then, Grey emerged from the barn. "I think we're good to go," he said.

The three of us walked back toward the bikes in silence. The collective tension we had all felt for the past few weeks was finally beginning to ease. This thing was far from over, but at least Hammer had finally been avenged. I thought about the thumb drive, and the Aztecs patch, and wondered what Lalo would say when we brought them to him.

CHAPTER 17

Cherish

"Surprise!"

I was still almost blind from the bright sunlight outside, but sitting at the table in front of me were Seton, Jules, and Monica. At the fourth, empty spot sat three brightly-colored bags with tissue paper coming out of the tops.

I stared at the three of them, not comprehending. I was just supposed to be meeting Seton for appetizers. "I don't understand…" I said dazedly.

"It's a surprise party, silly!" Jules laughed. "For you! To congratulate you on everything!"

"But…" I stammered as I looked down at the bags. "Is this for me?"

"Duh," Monica smiled, shaking her head. She stood and came toward me, enveloping me in a warm hug. Jules and Seton did the same. "Now," she said when they were finished, "sit down, order a drink and start opening!"

I did as she was told, still trying to recover from the surprise of seeing them all there. I had no idea what to make of all this. At the Ranch, we rarely received presents of any kind. Birthdays and other holiday celebrations were forbidden as being displeasing to God and rooted in paganism. So, to have the three women all make a special point of giving me presents, just because, almost brought me to tears.

"Thank you all, so much," I sniffed. "You really shouldn't have done this."

"Bullshit," Jules said firmly. "If there was ever a reason to celebrate, it's this. Look at everything that's happened to you in the last couple of months. It's amazing." The other women nodded their agreement.

Seton flagged down a waitress, and I ordered a Coke. "Nope," she said, her eyes twinkling. "A margarita." I smiled, remembering the first time we had met.

"So, open!" Monica said impatiently, pushing one of the bags closer to me. "This one's from me!"

Monica had gotten me a beautiful leather-bound journal and a container of what she said were called bath bombs. "The journal is so that you can write down the story of all the amazing things that you accomplish," she said. "Someday, when you have kids, they'll want to know the story of your life. And you have an amazing one. And the bath bombs are for relaxing in your bathtub when you get an apartment. Everyone needs a little pampering now and then."

Jules gave me a beautiful set of drinking glasses with intricate designs of flowers etched into the glass. "I wanted to get you something practical, yet beautiful," she said. I leaned over and hugged her, my eyes shining.

Seton's gift was the best of all, though. I reached into the bag and pulled out a beautiful forest-green dress, more elegant than anything I had ever owned in my life. "Seton," I breathed. "It's so beautiful!"

"Well, since I knew your size, I thought I would give you something that you probably would be too practical to buy yourself. And I knew that green would go perfectly with your hair."

I thanked them all again, trying not to choke up as I did so. Not long after, an order of nachos and a plate of quesadillas arrived with my drink, and we all dug in, chatting happily about everything and nothing.

"So, Cherish, are you any closer to finding an apartment?" Monica asked between bites.

"Not really. Seton has gone looking with me a couple of times. The problem is finding a place I can afford that's not either a closet or disgusting." I took a sip of my drink. "After my paycheck this week I have enough for a good security deposit, though, so at least I'll be ready when I do find something."

"Are you open to a roommate?" Jules asked. "I think my cousin might be looking for one soon."

Monica piped up. "Are you kidding? She needs a place of her own. So she and Levi can…" she raised her eyebrows suggestively.

Seton grinned. "Yeah, that's true! So," she said, scooting forward. "Spill it, Cherish. What's up with you and Levi? Have you talked about the *future* yet?"

At the mention of Levi's name, I stopped eating, suddenly feeling sick. "I, um…" I stammered and then cleared my throat. "I'm not sure we're together anymore. If we ever were," I said quietly.

"What?" Jules asked, sounding incredulous. "That's B.S."

"No, it's not," I shook my head. "He's been avoiding me ever since… well, he's been avoiding me for a little while now."

"Oh, come on," Monica scoffed. "That man is crazy about you. Are you sure you're not imagining things?"

I shook my head again. It was true. Levi had barely looked at me since the last night we had spent together. The next morning, he had already left by the time I woke up. I didn't see him all that day, and that night he didn't come up to the apartment. Or the next night. Or the night after that.

Seton must have seen how upset I was, because her face fell. "Oh, Cherish, I'm so sorry. I had no idea."

I started to tear up. "It's okay. You couldn't have known." I looked down into my drink. "I'm not really sure whether there was ever really anything between us, anyway." The idea that Levi had been just using me for sex made me want to throw up, but I had to consider that it was probably true. There was no other way I could explain his sudden distant attitude toward me.

"Well," Jules frowned. "There's other fish in the sea, after all, but I really thought Levi was into you."

"Oh, come on, he totally is!" Jules waved her hand dismissively. "Have you ever seen him look at anyone else that way? He is clearly crazy about her."

"How do you feel about him, Cherish?" Seton asked gently. "That's the important part."

"I…" I took a deep breath. "I've never felt like this about anyone before. He… when we're together… It's overwhelming. It's like all I want is to be next to him."

"What's the sex like?" Monica prodded.

"Monica!" Seton chided her.

"So, so amazing," I confessed. Somehow, it felt wonderful to be able to confide in these ladies about what it was like with Levi. "I mean, I guess I didn't know. Is it always like that? I've just never… you know…"

"Oh my gosh, were you a virgin until Levi?" Monica's eyes were wide.

"No, silly, she was married before," Seton frowned at her. "Remember?"

"Well, not legally," I corrected. "Thankfully."

"No kidding, if your hubby didn't know what to do in bed," Jules said drily. "And clearly, he did not."

"But yes, to answer your question, it is supposed to be 'like that,'" Seton affirmed. "With the right person, anyway. When Greyson and I first got together, our first time? Oh, my God, it was like I had never even had sex before, by comparison!"

Jules grinned and raised her eyebrows. "Repo's definitely brought out the kinky side of me, if you know what I mean."

The others laughed, and I blushed and looked down at my drink. I didn't know what Jules meant, exactly, but my body began to heat up at the thought of Levi teaching me new things. Until I remembered he was avoiding me, and my heart sank into my stomach.

"Cherish." I looked up at Seton to find her frowning at me in concern. "You okay?"

"I guess," I lamented. "I just wish he'd tell me if he didn't want me anymore."

"Oh honey, I can guarantee you that's not the problem," Monica laughed. "Have y'all seen the way he looks at her?" She fanned herself with her hand. "Lord, it's enough to give a girl heat stroke."

"Just be patient," Jules said. "The club's got a lot going on right now. All the men are distracted by it. And Levi's not the kind of man who's used to being tied down. He'll come around, though. Monica's right: the way he looks at you, no one could possibly doubt that he's smitten."

It touched my heart that all three of them were trying so hard to make me feel better. And judging from the way they talked, they truly seemed to believe what they were saying. But I wasn't convinced they knew any more about Levi's feelings than I did. If it was one thing I had learned about him, he didn't bare his soul to anyone. I knew that the things he had told me about his sister, and why he had left the WFZ Ranch, were things he had never confided to anyone else. I sure couldn't imagine him telling Seton or Jules — or anyone, for that matter — how he felt about us.

Even me, I thought miserably.

More drinks were ordered, more appetizers eaten, and more talk about anything and everything. Eventually my little surprise party wound down. I was on my bike, so Seton told me she'd put my presents in her car and bring them over to the clubhouse later. The three of them hugged me and congratulated me again, and we said goodbye in the restaurant parking lot.

I watched them drive off in their cars, bound for their own houses and their own families, and felt a pang of loneliness at the thought of going back to the little apartment and staring at the four walls. But even though the men of the MC would certainly be nice and humor me if I decided to linger in the clubhouse bar, I knew I'd just feel strange there, and even worse if Levi showed up and ignored me. Unlocking my bike, I straddled the seat and began the ride home with a heavy heart.

I was about a quarter mile away from the downtown area, on a winding and secluded stretch of the highway, when I heard a car coming toward me from behind. By now, I knew that sometimes people would hesitate to pass a biker in the road along this stretch because you couldn't always see around the corners. Instinctively, I pushed the bike over onto the shoulder and kept riding, waiting for the whoosh of wind and the blur of the car as it flew by. Instead, it slowed, and pulled behind me, so close that I could feel the heat of the engine on the backs of my legs.

A spike of fear shot through me, and the hair on the back of my neck literally stood up. *I didn't even know that really happened*, I found myself thinking absurdly. Not knowing what else to do, I kept riding, speeding up a little, and hoped that a car would come from the other direction so I could try to signal to it. No such luck, though. My breathing sped up as adrenaline began to course through my veins. Was whoever was behind me just trying to scare me? Or was something worse about to happen?

Suddenly, the vehicle gunned its engine and swerved out onto the highway, then pulled abruptly to a stop right in front of me, blocking my path. I was so startled I almost ran into it, and skidded to a stop with my tires inches from the passenger door. It was a large, black SUV with dark tinted windows. As I gaped at it and tried to tamp down my terror, the passenger window rolled down.

Isaiah Whitehead stared out at me.

"Thought you were clever, didn't you?" he sneered. I was paralyzed with fright as I watched him open the door and come to stand in front of me. He spat once, to his side, then before I knew what was happening, he stepped forward and backhanded me sharply across the face. "You ain't so clever."

The back of his hand had hit me squarely across the jaw and caught part of my ear as well. The force of the blow sent me staggering, the bike chain catching my ankle and biting into the skin as I fell onto the rough gravel. I sat for a moment, dazed, my ears actually ringing. *I didn't know that really happened, either*, I thought dimly.

I was staring down at the pavement, trying to clear my head, when I heard doors open on the other side of the SUV. Then I was being picked up roughly under the arms and pulled upwards. I cried out in pain as my hip connected solidly with something hard. Then I was flung onto something that must have been one of the seats. It was hard and smelled slightly of plastic fumes. The smell of a new or newish car. My hands were roughly bound behind me, then my legs pushed further into the seat.

A man I recognized as a cousin of Harlan Radleff got in beside me and slammed the door. "You best be quiet and behave," he rasped into my ear. "You give us any trouble, we got no reason to be kind to a little whore like you."

I awkwardly slid myself into more or less a sitting position, sliding away from the man as far as I could. My aching head came to rest against the cool window, and I could only close my eyes and try to breathe. The pounding in my ears made it hard to think, and anyway, there was nothing I could do with my hands bound against three men. I tried to take a few deep breaths, waited for my heart to stop slamming in my chest so frantically, and told myself that I'd try to think of something to do as soon as my head stopped hurting.

CHAPTER 18

Levi

Time was of the essence once we had disposed of Hook Nose's body and dumped the other two Cannibals by the side of the road a few miles into their territory. Grey sent word to Lalo that we needed an urgent meeting, and the next day we found ourselves following directions to what turned out to be an abandoned mine. There wasn't much in the way of above-ground structures when we got there, so we stood around sweating and getting baked by the sun, until eventually a large dark SUV limo pulled up and Lalo emerged, flanked by a phalanx of dangerous-looking men, some of whom I recognized from our last meet. There were only four of them, but I was sure there were others hidden somewhere not far off.

"To what do I owe the urgency of this meeting?" Lalo asked Grey in a calm voice.

It seemed unlikely that Lalo hadn't heard of our run-in with the Cannibals yet, but this was obviously how he was choosing to play it. For now.

"We have some new information that it was important to share with you in person," Grey responded. "It concerns the last conversation we had together."

"Please," Lalo said solicitously. "Continue."

Trig spoke up. "We told you we had a suspicion the recent attacks on our club were coming from the Cannibals."

"Yes," he nodded, looking a little impatient. "But you had no proof, as I recall."

"Not then. But we do now."

"You may have heard," Grey stepped in, "that

our clubhouse was pipe bombed a few days ago."

Lalo raised a brow. "No, I had not heard that. Most unfortunate. My condolences."

"No one was hurt." Grey continued as though Lalo hadn't spoken. "Not seriously, at least. But it turned out to be a blessing in disguise."

"How so?"

Trigger stepped forward, a tablet in his hand. "We have security cameras all around the clubhouse. One of them caught this." He held it out, and one of Lalo's men came forward and took it. Holding the tablet up to Lalo, he pressed play on the video that Trigger had called up. Lalo shaded his eyes with a hand as he watched the screen wordlessly for a minute. He looked up at Grey, then, his expression not changing.

"These men are Cannibals," he said. It wasn't a question. He clearly recognized them.

"Yes," Grey agreed. Trigger stepped forward and took the tablet back from Lalo's man. "Which, as we both know, is a clear violation of the truce between the Stone Kings and the Aztec cartel, since the Cannibals are now part of your organization."

For the first time, a flicker of emotion crossed Lalo's face. A tiny twitch of his jaw was all it was, but it was enough. Anger.

"The Aztecs have always honored our truce. This was not caused by us."

"I beg to differ," Grey countered. "They are part of your organization now. Which means that their actions, good or bad, reflect on you. There's more."

"What?" Lalo bit out through gritted teeth.

"We found this at the scene." Repo stepped forward this time, holding out the Aztecs patch so Lalo could see it. "The threads would indicate that it was ripped off a cut. Maybe by accident. Maybe on purpose."

"You think one of *my* men did this?" Lalo's voice had dropped a register. Cold, steely fury radiated from him unmistakably. This was where things would turn, one way or another.

"I'm not convinced," Grey shook his head. His tone was deliberately calm. "What I think is more likely, is that this was planted."

"Planted?"

"Lalo. You and I have always had a good professional relationship. You are a man of honor." Grey crossed his arms. "Our truce has been solid from the beginning. But Skull. The new president of the Cannibals. You said last time you don't know him all that well. Do you really think you can trust him?"

"Our relationship does not go back very far," he admitted grudgingly. "The negotiations for the Cannibals to join the cartel happened under the past president, Jimenez. Skull has said he would abide by the same negotiated agreement. But I will admit, he has seemed to… chafe under certain aspects of the deal between our organizations."

"Lalo, I would suggest to you that Skull may be trying to destabilize the partnership between us, with the larger goal of destabilizing you as leader of the cartel." Grey took a step forward. "I see no other good explanation for why we would find this patch at the scene of the explosion. No Aztecs were caught on camera, only Cannibals. I've come to you to ask you to work with us, and to give you this information as a gesture of good will toward the strength of our truce."

Lalo was silent for a long moment. No one said

anything; no one moved.

"Is this all?" he finally asked.

"No. I also came here to tell you that we tracked down and captured the three men in the surveillance video. During our interrogation, they confirmed that they had been responsible for the previous attacks on our club… and that one of them had been responsible for killing our brother Hammer." Grey's eyes were hard. "We ended him. We took our own justice, for Hammer's death."

Lalo's face was expressionless. "And the others?"

"We dumped them back in their territory. It's only a matter of time before they get back and tell Skull what happened."

A solid, agonizing minute passed as Lalo considered everything Grey had told him. Finally, Lalo set his jaw and spoke.

"So time is of the essence."

Grey nodded. "I'd say so."

Lalo turned to the men flanking him. "Bring Skull to me. Today." Then, to Grey. "May I keep the little memento you showed me?"

Repo stepped forward and handed the Aztecs patch to one of Lalo's henchmen.

Then it was Lalo's turn to step forward. "Grey. I hope that the issue of our truce has been resolved. I thank you for this information, and I trust that there will be no more attacks on the Stone Kings by members of our cartel."

Grey stuck out his hand and Lalo shook it. "I trust, as well." I let out my breath slowly, not realizing I had been holding it.

Lalo glanced briefly at all of us and nodded. "Gentlemen." He turned toward the SUV, his men following close behind. We watched in silence as they drove off.

"Fuck," said Trigger, relief in his voice. "Glad that's over."

"I expect we're gonna hear the Cannibals is under new management soon," Grey said drily. "Skull may be blissfully living out his final moments on earth right about now. Hope he's enjoying them." He turned to me and clapped me on the back. "Thanks for seeing clearly, Levi. This could have turned into something none of us wanted."

The mood was subdued but happy on the way back to the clubhouse. It was a relief to finally be able to shut the door on the last few months. Avenging Hammer couldn't bring him back, but it could at least bring some closure. And it was clear that once Lalo was through with Skull, he wouldn't be around to fuck with us anymore.

As I got closer to Lupine, my mind turned inevitably to Cherish, as it always seemed to when I wasn't working to keep myself occupied. I had been doing everything I could to avoid seeing her since our last night together, and it had been almost a week now since I had so much as had a conversation with her. I had thought it would get easier eventually — that after three or four days, I'd be able to stop thinking about her so much. But for some reason, tonight the pull toward her was almost more than I could take. All I could think about was finding her as soon as I got back to the clubhouse, taking her upstairs, and plunging myself deep inside her. I threw out a silent request to the universe that she wouldn't be there when I got back, so I could just have a quick beer with the men and ride home. But another part of me — the part that was half-sick in love with her — hoped that she would be there. Because that part of me knew damn well I wouldn't be able to resist her if she was.

It turned out the first part of me got its wish. But in the worst possible way.

I had just parked the bike and cut the engine when the door to the clubhouse opened and Seton came running outside. She spoke briefly to Grey, clutching his arm, and then ran to me.

"Levi," she began. Her eyes were wide, her face pale. "I think something might have happened to Cherish."

My veins turned to ice. "What? What do you mean?"

"Jules, Monica and I had a little surprise congratulations party for her at happy hour at the Luna. She was on her bike, so I took the presents we gave her in my car and came back here just now to bring them to her. But she's not here, and neither is her bike, and no one here has seen her since this morning."

"Holy shit." My eyes bored into hers. "And she hasn't called you or anything?"

"No, I checked my messages already. No calls, no texts."

I pulled out my phone with unsteady hands.

Nothing.

"Jesus Christ," I breathed. "Either strangers got her… or…"

"Or what?"

My blood ran cold in my veins. "Or the Ranch came for her."

CHAPTER 19

Cherish

My head was throbbing so painfully it was difficult to keep my eyes open. At first, I tried to pay attention out the window, to try to memorize the route the men were taking, but it was impossible to concentrate, so I gave up and let my eyes close and my head rest against the window. I told myself that anyway, it probably didn't make much difference whether I tried to pay attention right now.

I knew exactly where we were going.

When all three of the men had gotten back in the car and slammed the doors — causing a painful clanging in my head — I was roughly strapped into the seatbelt. "You try anything," Isaiah told me from the front seat, "You'll be even sorrier than you're already going to be when this is all over."

"Check her pockets," the driver barked. I hadn't been able to get a look at him yet, but his voice was so familiar... With a shock, I realized who it was.

"Elias?" I croaked in astonishment.

"You shut your mouth, Cherish. You just SHUT your mouth!" He turned in his seat and looked at me, rage evident in his flashing eyes. My brother was furious, in a way I had never seen or heard him be before. "You have brought disgrace down upon our home! You're nothing but a whore! You need the Devil beaten out of you, and that's exactly what you're going to get!" Angrily, he turned the key in the ignition and threw the car into gear with a clunk. The wheels squealed a little as he accelerated abruptly and made a jerky U-turn back toward town.

My heart began to pound hard in my chest as I thought of the few people who I had remembered escaping the Ranch when I was younger. I thought of how dead their eyes looked when they came back and were finally allowed to join the rest of us again. I had always wondered what had been done to them in their time of seclusion, and shuddered weakly now at the realization that I was about to find out.

The man beside me pushed me over onto one hip and checked my back pockets. "Cell phone," he muttered, pulling out the burner phone Seton had given me. He pushed the button to open the window and flung it out onto the road. My eyes pricked with sudden tears. The phone was the only way I had to contact anyone to come help me. Would I have been able to get a call or a text to Seton or Levi if he hadn't found it? Would the club have been able to track where I was with it? I would never know now. I'd be leaving Lupine just the way I'd arrived: with no money, no friends who knew where I was, and very little hope.

In spite of the pounding of my head, I must have slept, because suddenly I was being shaken awake by the man beside me. I raised my head painfully and looked out the window. We had stopped at an isolated rest area. "You need to put these on," he said, shoving a bundle of clothing toward me.

I saw that the other men had gotten out of the car and were standing outside, scanning the horizon for other vehicles. "I'm gonna get out of this car, and you're gonna change your clothes. You try anything, you're gonna be real sorry." Reaching behind me, he cut the plastic tie that had bound my hands. I moaned and rubbed my wrists as the circulation returned painfully.

The man — now that my brain was clearing a bit, I thought his name was Joseph — climbed out of the car and closed the door, but I noticed that his window was cracked just enough that he could see the top of my head. I sighed. There was no way I could do anything to try to get away now, so with a heavy heart, I separated the clothing he had given me. There were temple garments — the undergarments that members of all LDS sects wore — and a thick, heavy dress of the kind I had worn every day of my life until I'd escaped from the Ranch. Robotically, I donned the clothes, but left on the underwear I was wearing under them. The idea of these men seeing my intimate clothing filled me with revulsion. As I drew on the long, scratchy socks and slid my feet into the ill-fitting shoes, it was almost as though the last few months had never even happened. I stifled a sob that threatened to tear from my throat. Levi's face appeared, so vivid that I

could remember detail: his deep and penetrating
eyes, the scratchiness of his beard against my cheek,
the strong square jaw. I longed to see him again, to
feel that beard, to nestle into the crook of his arm.
The probability that I would never see him again was
unthinkable.

When I was finished dressing, Joseph took my
other clothing and threw it in the back of the SUV
with a sour look, as though he was touching filth.
The men got back in the car, and Isaiah looked at
me for the first time since they had taken me. A
disgusted grimace contorted his face. "Contain your
hair," he spat.

"I don't have anything to tie it back with," I said,
as calmly as I could. Only a trace of the fear spiking
through me came through in my trembling voice.

Joseph reached back to the clothing I had just
taken off, and grabbed my shirt. Violently, he tore it
along the bottom, rending it until he had a long strip
of fabric. "Here," he said tossing it at me. I did as I
was told, and tried to push down the unreasonable
sadness I felt at seeing one of the only remnants of
my former life being ripped to shreds.

We rode in silence for a long while, angry tension
so thick in the air it felt as though I would choke on

it. Eventually, Isaiah spoke.

"Did you really think I wouldn't find you, girl? Did you really think you'd get away that easily?"

I said nothing at first, afraid that anything I replied would be met with another slap to the face. Finally, I dared a question. "How did you? Find me?" I asked in a small voice.

"You can't survive out in Satan's garden without proof you're one of them," my brother Elias sneered contemptuously. "The second you had to get the record of your birth, the man you spoke to at the county courthouse got hold of us. Did you really think it would be that simple to disappear from us?"

Oh, God, no... I closed my eyes briefly in disbelief and regret. How could I have been so stupid to believe the man on the phone who told me he would help me? I realized with horror that when he had told me to send the application form directly to him, I was falling right into a trap. At his request, I had sent this stranger the form filled out with all the information Isaiah would need to find me in Lupine. Anger and frustration at how stupid I had been overwhelmed me, and silent tears began to stream down my face.

"So you went straight to a criminal who cavorts with the Beast," my brother spat with loathing. He meant Levi, I realized dimly. "Did you open your legs for him right away? Did you give yourself to him, defiling your body and making your flesh rotten like the filth that you are?"

I couldn't help but flinch at the violence in his words. "No," I whispered. "No." I wasn't denying that I'd slept with Levi, though they couldn't know that. But in my heart, I couldn't stand them saying that what had happened between Levi and me was wrong, or filthy. I knew I would probably never see him again. I knew that I had almost certainly lost him forever. But I could not and would not let myself be ashamed of what had happened between us. Let these men think what they wanted. Let everyone at the Ranch loathe and judge me. Inside, I would never let myself agree. I had been in love with Levi. I was *still* in love with Levi, I thought fiercely. And that made what had been between us beautiful. Even if he didn't feel the same. My love for Levi was *mine*. It was in *my* heart. And no one else could ever make it anything bad.

"What will happen to me?" I asked quietly.

"You will be punished," Isaiah retorted. "The

others in the community shall know what you have done. You will live in isolation, in penance, until you fully repent for all of your sins. When you rejoin the community, you will atone publicly, confess to all, and ask for forgiveness."

"Will… will I be going back to your home, Isaiah?" A tiny part of my heart jumped at the idea of seeing the children again. I had always tried to love them as well as I could, and I knew they had loved me. But the thought of Isaiah coming to my bed again in the night made me want to retch.

Isaiah turned and looked at me directly. There was no mistaking the loathing in his eyes. "I would not share a bed with a whore such as you. You shall be divorced from me. I doubt that any other man will want you, knowing what you have done. You will live out your days atoning for your sins and trying to correct the dishonor you have brought upon your family."

So I was to be brought back to the Ranch, only to be an outcast. Why, oh why hadn't they simply let me go? I thought desperately. I couldn't see any reason why they wouldn't have just written me off as a lost soul, like they had with Levi.

Levi…

With a lump in my throat, I leaned my forehead back against the window and stared at the landscape outside. The thumping of my head had lessened to a low throb, but the swelling of my cheek and mouth had started, leaving me with a different sort of pain.

Someday, I told myself. Someday, I would escape again. I'd be smarter this time. I would go somewhere else, somewhere completely new. I would change my name, cut all ties, and disappear. After a while, they would have to get sick of looking for me, and give up. I'd be like a ghost to them, and they would forget about me.

I'd be like a ghost for Levi, too. A tear rolled down my cheek, stinging my cut lip with its salt. Someday, it would be like I'd never even existed.

CHAPTER 20

Levi

I tried calling her burner, my fingers so shaky from adrenaline I could hardly punch the numbers. It went right to voice mail. "FUCK!" I screamed, and resisted the urge to throw my phone against the side of the clubhouse.

"What are we gonna do?" Seton asked, her eyes wide with panic.

Grey spoke. "First thing, ride the road she usually

takes coming home on her bike. Maybe she's got a flat and she's walking home."

"She would have been home at least an hour ago, even if she had to walk," Seton shook her head. "And I drove that road on the way here. No sign of her."

"Do you really think the people from... before... that they took her?" Seton whispered.

My jaw tensed in anger. "Yeah. I do." Something in my gut told me it was true. This wasn't some random bunch of thugs. The Ranch had found her, somehow. I didn't know how they'd done it. But I was pretty sure I knew what they would do to her now that they had her.

"We have to go after her." I turned to Grey. "She's not safe with them. They'll hurt her. Women aren't worth shit to them, they're just possessions. They'll treat her like a disobedient dog, beat her and tie her up so she won't run away again."

"Oh, my God. What do we do?" Seton asked.

"We know where they're going," I said. "Best thing is to catch up with them on the way, before they get back to the Ranch. The community has friends in the government and the police force up there. If they make it across the border before we overtake them, it'll be a lot harder to get her back."

"Okay." Grey nodded, thinking. "First, we need to ride the road she took, to look for any signs of her." He looked at me. "Take Repo and Cal. I'll have my phone. Call me if you find anything."

I headed out with the men a few minutes later, struggling to go slow on the bike so we could look for any signs. Cal and I found her bike in a ditch, abandoned but otherwise fine. Repo had ridden on a bit further, and a few minutes later he returned to where we were and held out the crushed remnants of a phone.

"Looks like it's been run over a couple of times," he said.

"Fuck." Cal shook his head.

"What do you want to do, brother?" Repo asked me. "You know the club is with you. We'll do whatever it takes to get her back."

"Let's go back to the clubhouse. We're gonna need a few more men." A thousand different emotions were swirling around in my head at once, primarily fear and anger. I let the anger take control. It was better that way. "We're gonna find her, and then we're gonna make sure those bastards never touch a hair on her goddamn head again."

There was only one road that would take you from Lupine to the town nearest to the WFZ Ranch with anything like a direct route. I had to assume that the men who had taken Cherish would follow it. *If they took her*, a voice said inside my head.

No. I couldn't let myself think about the possibility that it wasn't them. Because if I was wrong, if she hadn't been kidnapped by her Isaiah Whitehead and taken back to the Ranch…

Then I had no idea where she was. Which meant I had no way to save her.

One reason I'm the Sergeant at Arms of the Stone Kings is that I don't crack under pressure. I have long experience of keeping my emotions in check, keeping my cool in times of danger, and not letting anything show on my face that I don't want to show. But damned if I wasn't struggling with the adrenaline shakes as we set out to find Cherish. My normal ability to compartmentalize my emotions wasn't working in this case. I kept thinking of all sorts of things the WFZ men might be doing to her right now. None of the scenarios I was imagining were good. I wondered how she was doing: if she was terrified, if they had hurt her… My fist clenched tightly around the throttle as I imagined them touching her. Whatever they had done to her, once we found them, they would pay, and pay dearly.

There were ten of us, riding in formation as we sped down the one highway I was praying would lead me to Cherish. I glanced around at my brothers and felt a surge of gratitude for this family of men who always had my back. As soon as Cal, Repo and I had gotten back to the clubhouse and briefed the men, every single one of the Stone Kings had volunteered to come with us with no questions asked. Grey had some of the brothers stay behind to post guard just in case anything funny happened. Seton was at the clubhouse, and had called some of the other old ladies to stay and wait with her. She had assured me that she would call me or Grey right away if they heard anything at all.

Riding the speed limit, the trip from Lupine to the nearest town to the Ranch would take someone about seven hours, if they only stopped for gas and to piss. Seton told us that at the most, Cherish would have been gone about three hours. We flew out of Lupine at about thirty over the limit, increasing it to near forty on the open straightaways. Instead of our usual formation, I was riding in front on Grey's right, with Repo taking the spot I normally held as Sergeant at Arms. I needed to be able to see into vehicles as we passed, and communicate with Grey by hand signals if necessary, even though we had headsets as well.

It was frustrating as shit flying blind like this, especially because we had no idea what kind of car we were looking for, but as we came up on other vehicles, we fell into a routine of slowing down so that I could spend a few moments looking through the windshields to evaluate who and what was inside. The cars were fairly easy; it wasn't hard to see two parents with a couple of kids horsing around in the backseat, or a lone driver rocking out to the radio. I figured I was looking for at least two men, probably in a van or maybe something with dark windows, and probably Arizona plates, though I wasn't willing to bet on that. The WFZ men tended to wear a kind of uniform of long-sleeved button-down shirts in dark green, gray, or blue, so that was also something I was looking for. I didn't know if I'd see Cherish if she was in the car, so I wasn't necessarily looking for a woman. Since she had been abducted, she could be tied up in a backseat or — I tried not to think about it — even in a trunk.

Even as fast as we were flying along, every second was agonizing as my brain went in circles trying to figure out if there was anything that could tell me where Cherish was right now. In the back of my mind, was the nagging thought, cold and lethal as a dagger: what if we were on completely the wrong track? What if Cherish hadn't been taken by the men of the Ranch, and by the time we figured that out, it was too late?

For the hundredth time I pushed the thought away. *No.* It wasn't possible. Somehow, I knew, almost more strongly than I'd ever known anything, that if something had already happened to Cherish — if someone had hurt her, even killed her — I would *feel* it. I would know it in my gut. A world without her in it was unimaginable. She was a light that couldn't just *go out,* just like that, without… I don't know, without some sort of earthquake, or tidal wave, or something.

If she was gone, if someone took her — took her *from me* — how could life just continue? How would my heart just fucking continue to *beat*, like nothing had happened? No, I told myself firmly. It wasn't possible. We *would* find her. And it would not be too late.

All the effort I had made to try to stay away from Cherish in the last days, all the work I had put into trying to tell myself I could just let her go and get over her — I saw now that it had all been a fucking ridiculous game I had been playing with myself. I could no more leave Cherish alone than I could fly to the goddamn moon by flapping my arms. Ever since the first day I had seen her in the parking lot of the clubhouse, I had been a goner. I pictured her now, in that ridiculous damn Minions shirt that I would give everything I owned to see her in again. My throat closed up at the memory, and I swallowed painfully. Next to me, Grey must have heard the low, strangled sound I had made in my throat through his headset, because he turned to look at me and cocked his head. "You good?" he asked. I nodded but said nothing, not trusting my voice.

I wasn't a religious man. It was hard to be, after everything I'd seen growing up. But as I ate up the highway on my bike with my brothers next to me, I found myself thinking that if God did exist, He wouldn't let anything happen to Cherish. She was too good, too brave, too beautiful. Almost without meaning to, I sent up a silent prayer. *If you are out there, don't take her from me. I won't let her go again.*

We'd been riding for a couple of hours when we came up on the approach of a small town. A few buildings on the outskirts faced the highway, to lure in people passing through with gas and food. As we had agreed to, the formation stopped about half a mile from the first buildings, so as not to attract attention. Grey and I went ahead to see what we could see. We approached a truck stop that had a small restaurant and a small grocery-convenience store. We parked the bikes at the furthest gas pump from the store and pretended to get ready to fill our tanks. I was scanning the large trucker parking lot to the left of the store when Grey lightly tapped me on the shoulder. "Hey," he said.

I glanced over in the direction of his gaze. Coming out one of the side doors of the convenience store was a man in a dark blue shirt and black pants. Behind him, another man in a gray shirt followed, holding the arm of a woman. She wore a light blue dress made of heavy fabric, and her head was down.

Cherish.

CHAPTER 21

Cherish

After a while, I had to pee pretty badly, and pulled together my courage to ask for a rest stop. Isaiah gruffly refused, saying I could wait until they needed to stop for food and gas. When I told him I was likely to lose control in the car, the man next to me slapped me roughly across the face and told me to shut up. I sank down into the seat and tried desperately to think of anything else but my bladder.

About half an hour later, relief flooded through me as we pulled off the road at a gas station and convenience store that appeared at what looked to be the outskirts of a small town. Joseph pulled me out of the car, and I scrambled to keep up so I wouldn't fall on the ground before I got my legs under me. Once I was out, he jerked up on my arm, causing a slice of pain to shoot from my shoulder. I did my best not to cry out.

"No stupid tricks," he rasped against my ear. "You try anything in there and you'll be sorrier than you ever have been."

I knew that since Isaiah was planning to divorce me once we got back to the Ranch, I could not count on any level of kindness from any of them. I was disposable to them all now; the only reason they had come to get me was pride, and to punish me. I took a deep shuddering breath and nodded, but said nothing as he led me toward the store, his fingers digging into my upper arm.

Inside was a bright, fluorescent blur of food packages and beeping machines. I saw a couple of people casting curious looks at us, and for the first time felt how out of place I really was in the clothing I had grown up in. Now that I had been away, and had a taste of life outside of WFZ, I realized that to the other customers in the store, I was little more than a curiosity. Their eyes traveled to my strange clothing and clunky shoes, but their gazes never met mine. I felt more isolated from them now that I had actually had a life in Lupine. My mind cried out to them, to ask them to help me, but I knew they would never notice that the man holding my arm was doing so against my will. Inside these clothes, I was invisible.

Joseph led me through the store towards a bathroom at the back. "Make it quick," he growled, and stood at the entrance, making sure no one else would be able to enter or talk to me. I went inside and locked myself in a stall, exhaling in relief as I finally was able to empty my bladder. I sat there, staring blindly at the graffiti on the stall door, alone for the first time since the men had captured me. A shudder of grief and fear passed through me, and I began to sob as quietly as I could, tears streaming down my face.

About a minute later, a loud rap on the door reminded me that Joseph was waiting. Hastily, I pulled up my underwear and rearranged my temple garments and my clothing. I emerged from the stall and went to wash my hands. As I did so, I looked up in the mirror. A near-stranger stared back at me, as if she were a woman I used to know but hadn't seen in many years. Dejectedly, I splashed some water on my face and dried it off with paper towels, then opened the door and allowed myself to be led out of the store and back to the SUV.

Isaiah and Elias got back in the car, having filled the tank with gas, and we set off again. I could see by the changing landscape that we were getting closer to the Arizona border. Every second, every rotation of the tires took me closer to the life I had risked everything to escape. I closed my eyes again and leaned back, too exhausted to think or cry anymore. It was no use struggling, no use hoping. It was too late.

Suddenly, from the front seat Elias swore, and my eyes flew open. I had never heard a man of the WFZ swear before. He said something low and angry to Isaiah, who leaned over to look in his side mirror. At first I didn't know what was causing their reaction, but then, off in the distance, I heard a low rumble that I couldn't quite make out. As it got louder, I cocked my head listening, until finally, I realized what it was.

Motorcycles. A lot of them.

The men began to shout and argue, and the car swerved sharply as Elias turned to respond to an order from Isaiah. Joseph had bound my hands again once we had left the convenience store, this time in the front, and I tried awkwardly to brace myself against the driver's seat as the SUV briefly left the road for the shoulder. Elias swerved back onto the pavement, and floored the gas, trying to outrun the approaching bikers, but he was too late: A line of them quickly overtook him, surrounding him to the front and the side and forcing him off the road. Elias swore again as we went down a small embankment, and I shrieked involuntarily, sure the car was going to roll over. Finally, we skidded to a stop in the sand about ten feet from the highway. The bikes quickly circled us from all sides.

"Get the fuck out of the car!" a voice I recognized yelled. It was Grey, and the tone of fury in his voice made me remember what Seton said about how he could terrify grown men.

Isaiah leaned forward and reached for the glove compartment. I realized with a flash of terror what he was about to do, and screamed "GUN!" at the top of my lungs. Instantly, the passenger door opened and a large handgun was pointing at Isaiah's head. "I don't *fucking* think so," a voice spat.

Levi!

"Get out of the goddamn car. NOW." Levi's voice snarled. Without waiting for an answer, he grabbed Isaiah's arm and pulled with such force that he fell out of the car onto the ground. "You. First rule is you do not fucking talk unless I tell you you can talk. Got that?"

I couldn't see Isaiah now, but I assumed he must have agreed, because Levi nodded once. "Good." He peered into the car. "Driver. You get your ass out here. Hands up." The door opened from the outside, and Elias stepped out of the car without a word, hands high.

The rear passenger door opened then, and Trig's face appeared. "Three men to take down one small woman?" he clucked sarcastically when he saw Joseph. "You fuckers are even bigger pussies than I thought." He chuckled once, then a mask of fury settled over his face. "Get out of the fucking car, you piece of shit."

Joseph did what he was told. As he walked away from the car, Trig gave him a violent shove, then turned back to look inside at me. "How you doin' darlin'?" He asked. "They hurt you?"

I realized that at some point I had started trembling like a leaf. "No, not much," I replied shakily.

He looked down at my hands. "Let me get that off of you." Leaning forward, he reached into a pocket and brought out a knife, which he opened with a flick of his thumb. He severed the plastic with one efficient swipe, then held out a hand to help me from the car. "Come on out, now," he said in a soothing voice. "Everything's over."

I shakily stepped down from the SUV, almost stumbling. Trig caught me easily and helped me get to my feet. Wordlessly, I gave him a grateful look, and he nodded once, then lifted his chin to my left. I looked up to see Levi standing there, a million different emotions in his eyes. I stifled a sob and ran to him, and he caught me and lifted me up in his arms. "Cherish. You're safe," he whispered against my neck. "You're safe, baby. I got you."

Levi put me down gently, and nodded for me to go back and stand next to Trig. I stood silently, still trying to quiet my trembling, and watched the scene unfolding in front of me. Isaiah, Elias, and Joseph were all backed up against the side of the SUV, their hands in the air. Grey, Repo, and Winger all had their guns trained on them.

Trig leaned down to me and said quietly. "You

may not want to watch this, Cherish." He took me gently by the arm to lead me away but I shook my head. "No," I said stubbornly. "I want to stay." I had been the reason that the Stone Kings had come here. I couldn't just shy away from the consequences.

Levi stepped forward toward the three men, stopping in front of my former husband. "You Isaiah Whitehead?" he asked. Isaiah nodded but didn't say a word. "You recognize me?" Again, Isaiah nodded.

"Good." Levi took another step forward, and grabbed hold of his windpipe. Isaiah's eyes went wide, and he began to struggle for breath. Levi continued talking as though nothing was wrong. "Are you the one who organized this little adventure to come find Cherish?" Isaiah choked and struggled. "Answer me, motherfucker. Are you?" Isaiah began to turn a bright red. He nodded his head rapidly, his hands lowering to try to break Levi's choke hold. I closed my eyes and turned away for a moment, but forced myself to turn back.

"Here's the thing," Levi continued conversationally. "Cherish doesn't want to go back to the Ranch. Do you, Cherish?" he asked, looking at me.

I shook my head. "No," I said, making my voice as strong and as calm as I could.

"There. You see? Cherish doesn't want to go back. Did you ask her whether she wanted to go back when you picked her up?" Isaiah's face was purple now, and his thrashing was getting weaker. "Here. I want to hear you say it." Levi removed his hand from the man's throat, and Isaiah sank to the ground, coughing and gasping. He retched, on his hands and knees, a string of saliva snaking from his mouth.

"I asked you a question," Levi repeated patiently. "Did you ask Cherish if she wanted to go back to the Ranch?"

"No," Isaiah coughed, his voice a rough rasp.

"Well, then. There's your problem. You should fucking ask a woman what she wants before you just assume. Shouldn't you?"

Isaiah didn't answer. Before I realized what was happening, Levi's boot came out, kicking Isaiah in the jaw. I gasped, my hands flying to my mouth. "*Shouldn't you?*" Levi demanded, all pretense of calm gone now as he roared his anger at the man who had abducted me.

"Yes," Isaiah whimpered. He shook his head slightly and spit. Blood pooled onto the sand below.

"Okay then," Levi said, his voice once again a model of calm. He stepped forward and grabbed Isaiah by the hair, pulling him up into a standing position. He threw him back against the SUV. "Now. I want you to look at Cherish."

Isaiah's eyes met mine, a terrifying mixture of fear and fury.

"This is where you apologize to her."

"I'm sorry," Isaiah whispered.

"Good. Now." Levi turned and spread his arm, indicating the Stone Kings. "These men here. They are my brothers. They are my family. And they, unlike you motherfuckers, are not a bunch of cowardly pieces of shit who have to beat women into submission. But damned if they don't enjoy a good beatdown. And I can tell they are itching to end you motherfuckers. So you're lucky that I'm feeling charitable today."

Levi turned back to Isaiah, and grabbed him by

the collar, pulling him up until they were at eye level with each other. "If you ever, ever, try to so much as talk to Cherish again," Levi said in a voice as cold as steel, "these men, with me at the front of the pack, will hunt the three of you down and kill you. Do you hear me? We will kill you. Do you believe me?"

He looked at each of the men in turn, and waited for each of them to nod.

"Good." Still holding on to Isaiah's collar, he threw him down into the sand in one fluid motion. "Now, you miserable bastards, get the hell out of my sight. I don't ever want to see or hear about you again in this state."

Isaiah scrambled up out of the sand, wiping his bloodied nose, and the three of them got quietly into the SUV. None of them dared to look at me or any of the men as they shut their doors, started the engine, and drove slowly back onto the road. We all watched in silence as they retreated into the distance, finally disappearing over the horizon.

When they were gone, I looked up to see Levi standing at my side. "Fuck," he breathed, raising his hand to my face. "You're hurt."

"I'll be okay." I shook my head. "Just bruised,

mostly."

Softly, he stroked my swollen lip with my thumb. "Cherish," he murmured, his eyes shining. "Jesus. I'm so sorry."

"Why are you sorry?" I asked in confusion.

He sighed, then wrapped me in his arms, kissing the top of my head.

"The whole ride here, I was promising myself that when I got you back safe, I'd never let you go again," he murmured into my hair. "I'm sorry I ever tried to let you go in the first place. I was trying to let you make your own life, your own decisions. I was trying to stay out of your way." He pulled back, and looked at me, his eyes burning with intensity. "I love you, Cherish. I want you to be mine. Forever. But it's your decision. I don't want to stand in the way of your future."

"Of course it's my decision," I said, laughing softly. "And I already told you. I'm yours. I love you, Levi. I can't imagine being with anyone else."

He lifted my chin and kissed me deeply, instantly awakening the familiar heat and longing deep inside me. I moaned softly and returned his kiss, our tongues dancing eagerly. When he pulled away, I looked dizzily up into his eyes, and then suddenly remembered we weren't alone. My glance darted to the other men, who had wandered off toward their bikes, trying to pretend they couldn't see us.

"I think we're causing a scene," I said, smiling up at him.

"I think you're right. You okay to ride?" he asked softly.

"Well," I said, looking down at the heavy dress I was wearing, "I think I can make it back into town, but I'm going to need a change of clothes."

"Let's go see what we can find," he replied, his eyes twinkling. "Maybe they have a Minions shirt."

CHAPTER 22

Levi

All the drama in our little world vanished as quickly as it had come. The brothers and I brought Cherish back to Lupine that night, and life went back to normal.

The men from the Ranch never bothered her again.

The Stone Kings didn't hear anything directly about what had gone down between Lalo and the Cannibals, following our revelations about who had been responsible for the attacks. But we did get a communiqué, of sorts. One day, an envelope arrived at the clubhouse, with no return address and no postage. One of the men brought it to Grey, who opened it in front of me and a few of the others.

Inside, was the Aztecs patch that Grey had given to Lalo. The smears of blood on it told us all we needed to know.

Now that I was no longer trying to hide my love for Cherish, from her or from myself, things progressed pretty quickly between us. Every day, she got more beautiful to me, and the more I watched her make a life for herself, the prouder I was of her. Even though I wanted her with me every second of every day, I did at least try to give her some space, so I wouldn't suffocate her.

We talked about her moving in with me right away, but I told her she should get an apartment by herself for a while until she was absolutely sure. She fought me on it, but she finally agreed to a month to month lease on a nice little furnished studio near downtown. Turned out, it was a waste of money. We ended up spending every night together, anyway, and after three months she finally wore me down and made me realize I should stop trying to give her room and just move her into my place.

Cherish's twenty-second birthday was the week after the Stone Kings had rescued her from Isaiah and the WFZ. I knew she didn't think I knew about it, and I wouldn't have known the date at all if I hadn't been the one to take her to the courthouse that first day.

To tell the truth, I wasn't even sure she would remember it on the actual day, either. Birthdays were never acknowledged at the Ranch, so it was easy to forget about them when you had grown up there. But I had decided that it was going to be my ongoing job to make up for the first twenty-one she never celebrated. And tonight was step one in that plan. I'd even conspired with her manager at Hammie's to give her the night off, knowing that it would never occur to Cherish to request it.

I made up some pretext for taking her out for a night on the town, saying that since she'd never officially been on a date before, it was high time that she went on one. I told her we were going to someplace fancy, so she needed to dress up. I even borrowed a cage from one of the other brothers so she wouldn't have to ride on the back of my bike in a dress.

I arrived at the clubhouse wearing a dark button down shirt and dark jeans, leaving my leather cut at home for once. I suffered through the hoots and jeers of the men, until Cherish appeared at the top of the stairs, wearing a form-fitting dark green dress that actually, literally took my fucking breath away. Her hair hung loose and wavy around her shoulders, the way I liked it, and the dress hugged her hips and her breasts so perfectly that my dick hardened in my pants at the knowledge that in a few hours, I'd be sliding my hands over the smooth fabric, pushing her skirt up to find the treasure that was waiting for me underneath.

I kissed her once, deeply, then escorted her to the car, holding the door open for her as she got in. She seemed a little overwhelmed by all the attention, and I felt like a king for being able to do this one simple thing and be the first man (the *only* man, I told myself) to ever do something like this for her.

The restaurant I took her to had outdoor seating,

and we sat under the stars as I watched Cherish ponder the menu like it was a life or death decision. When she'd chosen, the waiter left and returned a moment later with a bottle of champagne I'd asked for when I made the reservations. I'd only had champagne once before in my life, and I wasn't much for it, but I would have bought fifty bottles of it just to hear the way Cherish laughed when she tried it.

"It tickles!" she smiled. "It feels like I'm going to sneeze!"

She took another sip and laughed again, then set it down. "Levi, what is all this? What's the occasion?"

"Happy birthday," I said, setting a small box down in front of her.

Her eyes grew wide. "Is… How did you know? I don't understand!"

"You told the county clerk your birthday the day I took you down to the courthouse," I said simply.

"And you remembered that all this time?"

I nodded. "Did you remember it was your birthday?"

"Um, sort of," she said vaguely, shrugging. "But… you know."

"Yeah. I know." I did. Even all these years after leaving the Ranch, I had never celebrated my own birthday. It just hadn't ever occurred to me.

"So, all this…" she said, nodding down at the champagne and the box in front of her, "This is because of my birthday?"

"Yep," I grinned. "So get ready, because I'm gonna pamper the shit out of you every year."

"Levi," she said softly, her eyes shining. "I love you so much."

"I love you, too, babe," I said, my voice husky. "Now, open your present."

A few days before, I had gone to a local jewelry maker with a rush job for an idea I had. The result was inside the box.

"Oh, Levi," Cherish said quietly as she took it out. "I…" Her voice broke. "Thank you so much!"

It was a gold necklace, with a simple pendant the jewelry maker had designed especially for Cherish: a C and an L, intertwined together.

"I wanted to give you something so you'll always know. Not just that you're mine. That I'm yours. For as long as you'll have me," I said.

For a moment she just looked down at her plate, and I could tell she was having trouble speaking. When she finally looked back up at me, her eyes were shining. "It's so beautiful, Levi," she whispered. "It's perfect. You're perfect." She looked around the restaurant, and started to laugh, as two tears fell from her eyes. "My God, I'm so happy! I never knew anyone could be this happy!"

"Me neither, babe," I said, as I fought to keep my composure. "Me neither."

Later that night, I took her back to my place. I made love to her long and slow. It seemed like we'd never get enough. I knelt between her legs and worshipped her with my tongue until she bucked against me. She knelt at the foot of the bed and took me in her mouth, making me groan with pleasure and trying as hard as I could not to lose control like a fucking virgin. When I was getting close and tried to push her away, she refused, telling me it was her birthday and she was claiming her second present. Then, her full, pouty lips wrapped back around my cock, just like I had fantasized about the first day I met her, and she brought me to a shuddering release as I came so hard I thought I might pass out.

We slept for a little while, and when I woke, it was the middle of the night, and I was curled around her, my dick hardening against her beautiful ass. I groaned and pulled her tighter to me, and she woke up and shifted in my arms to look at me. Wordlessly, we kissed, her breathing speeding up as my tongue probed deep into her mouth. Soon, she was whimpering and pressing her wet pussy against my cock. "Levi," she whispered urgently. "I need you."

Moonlight was streaming in through the window, and I suddenly wanted more than anything to see her beautiful body. I rolled on my back and pulled her on top so she was straddling me. It was the first time she had ever been on top, and she blushed furiously as I looked up at her. Then, with a wicked smile that caught me completely by surprise, she raised herself up and sank slowly down onto my throbbing cock. She closed her eyes and began to move with me inside her, sliding up and down, her mouth parted in pleasure. I reached up and brushed my thumb against her lips, and she took it in her mouth sucking on it as her tongue licked the pad. I groaned deeply, and she leaned forward, changing the angle so that her wet slit was rubbing against the top of my shaft as she rode me.

"Levi," she panted. "I'm getting close."

Jesus Christ. The sound of her saying my name, taking her pleasure, was almost more than I could bear. I took my thumb from her mouth and slid it against the hard nub of her nipple, causing her to gasp. Her eyes opened, finding mine, and she moaned, moving faster up and down. I could feel her pussy begin to squeeze me, and I knew it wouldn't be long. We rode the wave together, locking eyes, until finally she threw back her head and cried out, her pussy pulsing around me as she came. It was all I needed, and with a roar, I joined her, emptying myself inside her as she milked me dry.

Afterwards, I lay awake in the dark and listened to the sound of Cherish's calm, rhythmic breathing as she slept beside me. I thought about what an irony it was that the past I had tried so hard to leave behind me had come crashing back into my life, bringing with it the one woman I would never be able to live without. I had thought the Stone Kings would be the only family I would ever need, or want, but I was wrong. The future wouldn't mean anything to me without Cherish in it. I looked forward to watching her take her place in the world, and I was going to do everything I could to cheer her on and make sure nothing stood in her way.

And then, once she had had plenty of time to choose a life for herself, I was going to marry the shit out of her.

I looked over at her sleeping form, resisting the urge to wrap my arms around her and wake her up. Instead I lay back and folded my hands behind my head. I closed my eyes and began to feel the tug of sleep pull me under, knowing for once that no matter what happened, no matter what lay in store for Cherish and me tomorrow, we were both exactly where we needed to be.

THE END

Books by Daphne Loveling

Motorcycle Club Romance

Los Perdidos MC

Fugitives MC

Throttle: A Stepbrother Romance

Rush: A Stone Kings Motorcycle Club Romance

Paranormal Romance

Untamed Moon

ABOUT THE AUTHOR

Daphne Loveling is a small-town girl who moved to the big city as a young adult in search of adventure. She lives in the American Midwest with her fabulous husband and the two cats who own them.

Someday, she hopes to retire to a sandy beach and continue writing with sand between her toes.

Printed in Great Britain
by Amazon